GLASS SLIPPERS

SISTERS EVER AFTER

GLASS SLIPPERS

Leah Cypess

DELACORTE PRESS

Text copyright © 2022 by Leah Cypess
Jacket art copyright © 2022 by Kelsey Eng

Delacorte Press is a registered trademark and the colophon is a trademark of Penguin Random House LLC.

Visit us on the Web! rhcbooks.com

Educators and librarians, for a variety of teaching tools, visit us at RHTeachersLibrarians.com

Library of Congress Cataloging-in-Publication Data
Names: Cypess, Leah, author.
Title: Glass slippers / Leah Cypess.
Description: First edition. | New York : Delacorte Press, [2022] |
Series: Sisters ever after ; book 2 | Audience: Ages 9–12. | Summary: "When Tirza is accused of stealing Queen Ella's glass slippers, she must find the true culprit before the King and Queen lose their patience"— Provided by publisher.
Identifiers: LCCN 2020054100 (print) | LCCN 2020054101 (ebook) |
ISBN 978-0-593-17887-4 (hardcover) | ISBN 978-0-593-17889-8 (ebook)
Subjects: CYAC: Sisters—Fiction. | Characters in literature—Fiction.
Classification: LCC PZ7.C9972 Gl 2022 (print) | LCC PZ7.C9972 (ebook) | DDC [Fic]—dc23

The text of this book is set in 12.5-point Golden Cockerel ITC Std.
Interior design by Carol Ly

Printed in the United States of America
10 9 8 7 6 5 4 3 2 1
First Edition

To Tikva
The best of youngest sisters

⇒ PROLOGUE ⇐

I didn't do it.

I know you don't believe me. I can hardly blame you. So why do I even bother saying it?

I guess I've been saying it for so long that I've gotten into the habit. And I'm going to keep saying it, over and over, until I find *someone* who doesn't think I'm a liar and a thief.

Of course, that would have to be someone who doesn't know me. Who hasn't heard the story of my family, and how they treated Cinderella, and how they were punished for it.

Who hasn't seen the evidence and realized that every bit of it points to one conclusion: I'm the one who stole the queen's glass slippers.

Most of you were expecting something like this from me. The third stepsister, the one not even mentioned in most of the stories. I was, after all, only a baby when my mother married Cinderella's father, and only five years old when Cinderella went to the ball and caught the eye of the prince. Nobody could blame me for the things my family had done to her.

That was what Cinderella said when she exiled my sisters but welcomed *me* into the castle.

Everyone else knew better. It was inevitable, they said, that I would grow up as wicked as my two other sisters. It was a miracle I didn't reveal my true nature until I was eleven years old.

Given what happened, I can't exactly claim they were *wrong*. But they weren't one hundred percent right either.

Let me start at the beginning and see if I can make you understand. About the glass slippers and the godmother's plan and how everything went dreadfully wrong. Maybe you'll forgive me; maybe not. That's up to you.

But there's one thing I really, really need you to believe.

I didn't do it.

1

My original plan for that day was *excellent*. It doesn't mean much now, but for the record, I want you to know how well things could have gone.

It was the morning of the annual parade. I planned to spend the day in the nursery playing with the royal princes. Queen Ella's children, Prince Baro and Prince Elrin, were also not allowed to go to the parade. They had begged me to come stay with them, and I had promised.

I would never break a promise to the princes. Even that time when I told Baro that if he went to sleep, I would sing him the entire ballad of *Sleeping Beauty* while standing on my head. I hadn't thought he would remember, but he had, and I'd done it. Gilma, their nursemaid, had caught me and told everyone, which had gone over really well with the court.

But the princes were the only people in the castle

who trusted me, and I would never do anything to betray that trust.

So even when I got close enough to the nursery to hear the wailing, I kept walking. I slowed down a little bit, I admit. I might have winced. But I didn't stop.

"I *want* to go to the parade!" That was Baro, who, at five years old, had perfected the art of the tantrum. "It's not fair! Everyone in the whole world gets to do what they want except me!"

A thud, a crash, and another set of wails—these coming from one-year-old Elrin. I quickened my step, which made me trip on a loose section of the rug. I caught myself against the wall and kept going.

"I'm a *prince*! That means I can do whatever I want!"

I broke into a jog and wrenched the nursery door open, just in time to see Baro dump a bottle of purple glitter over his little brother's head.

"Baro!" Gilma cried. "Oh, don't do that!"

Baro grabbed a jar of glue.

"No, no, no." Gilma wrung her hands. "That's not how a prince should behave!"

Elrin yowled, grabbed a chunk of his older brother's hair, and yanked. Baro shrieked.

"Stop fighting!" Gilma wailed. "What would your subjects think?"

I strode into the room, grabbed Elrin's hand, and

disentangled it from Baro's hair. Then I held Elrin out of his brother's reach. Glitter rained down from his clothes, covering me with purple sparkles.

"I have a *great* idea," I said. "Once you stop screaming, I'll tell you all about it."

While I was waiting Baro out, I calmed Elrin down by giving him a sweet pop. He nuzzled into my shoulder and sucked happily, drizzling sticky saliva down the side of my neck.

"He shouldn't be having sweets, Tirza," Gilma said.

I gave her a look. She gave me a look right back, then held a hand out to Baro. "Do you want to help me clean up? I'll let you hold the dustpan."

Baro grabbed my skirt and buried his face in it. Gilma's mouth twisted. She went and got a broom and dustpan from the corner.

I thought about offering to help. Gilma, like me, had an odd position at court: She was a village girl who had been hired long ago as a nursemaid, but she was also given gowns and her own room and allowed to attend banquets and balls when the princes were asleep. That had caused a lot of muttering at court, but eventually, everyone had concluded that it was evidence of the queen's sweetness and good nature. After all, Queen Ella had once been a commoner, too, just like Gilma.

And like me.

So there had been a time—a brief time—when Gilma and I had been close. Cinderella had suddenly become too busy being queen to spend time with me, and Gilma had been like a replacement older sister. But she had quickly realized that it was bad enough being a commoner in fancy clothes without also having the queen's wicked stepsister glued to her side. It hadn't taken her long to join the noblewomen in their whispers and sneers. Then one day, when I was seven years old, she had poured green dye into my hair while two noble girls held me down. They had laughed and laughed. Even more than I remembered the humiliation of walking around with green hair, I remembered the pure delight in Gilma's laugh.

Gilma had been banned from the ball that year, and instead was forced to spend the evening emptying all the castle chamber pots. Ever since then, she had hated me.

By the time Gilma had finished cleaning the glitter (well, most of it—there is glitter in that room to this day), Baro had calmed down. "What's your idea?" he demanded. "Are we going to the parade?"

"Certainly not!" Gilma snapped. "Bad enough that you keep sneaking into your mother's room. Do you know who gets in trouble when you don't stay where you belong? *I* do, that's who."

Baro's lower lip jutted out, and his eyes welled up with tears.

"I have something better!" I said quickly. I knelt in front of Baro—which, unfortunately, meant I put my knee down in an unnoticed patch of glitter. And this dress was almost new; the laundress was going to hate me even more than she already did. "Do you know how *hot* it is, standing outside in the sun to watch a parade? I would rather be here."

Gilma snorted. "Convenient, since *you're* definitely not allowed to go."

She wasn't wrong, but she also wasn't helping.

"I'm sad to miss the parade too," Gilma went on, stretching her arms above her head. "But at least I have the ball to look forward to, and that's just three nights away. The queen gave me a new gown, and it's absolutely gorgeous. It's too bad you won't get to see it, Tirza."

I kept my eyes on Baro, lowering my voice. "Let's stay here and make an obstacle course."

Tears spilled onto Baro's chubby cheeks. "I hate obstacle courses!"

"Why?"

"I don't know," Baro said. "What's an obstacle course?"

While I explained, Gilma hopped onto the windowsill, straining to get a glimpse of the parade. Which wasn't going to happen; the parade was on the opposite side of the castle. I chose not to explain that to her.

Half an hour later, Gilma *still* hadn't caught on, but at

least she stayed out of the way of our obstacle course. She kept her face pressed to the glass, contorting her body to try to see from different angles, muttering, "*Why* do these things never start on time?" and "Did I miss it already? It's your fault for distracting me."

"What," a voice from the doorway demanded, "are you doing?"

Gilma turned so fast that she overbalanced, fell off the windowsill, and landed face-first onto the blanket hammock that Baro had been carefully setting up for the past ten minutes. He stared at his ruined construction, let out an outraged wail, then broke down and sobbed.

Elrin, who was watching me tie ropes across the top of the cradle, blinked. His lower lip trembled.

He burst into a loud, delighted laugh.

Baro grabbed a pillow and threw it at his brother. It missed and hit me instead.

Gilma glared at me as if this were *my* fault.

Meanwhile, the person whose fault it *actually* was stood in the doorway. He crossed his arms over his chest. "I guess the question should be what *were* you doing?"

"It's an obstacle course." I went to pick up Baro, stepping over a maze of wooden blocks. "Well. It was an obstacle course."

"Whatever you say." Aden raised his bushy eyebrows as he surveyed the room. He was wearing his court clothes, the ones he put on when he was selling cupcakes to the nobility—gray trousers that were a tiny bit too long on him and a white tunic embroidered with gold thread. I guessed that his regular clothes were being washed and that was why he wasn't at the parade. He had only one set of nice clothes, and he couldn't risk getting them dirty.

"It *was* a mess, and now it's an even worse mess," Gilma snapped, glaring at him.

Aden winked at me. "I'm bored. Come to the northern battlements?"

Baro was still wailing into my shoulder—which was now soaked with his tears—and Elrin looked like *he* was going to cry because I had abandoned him. I shook my head.

"What's on the northern battlements?" Gilma demanded.

The answer was an *actual* view of the parade. Of course, Gilma couldn't leave the princes unattended, but what if we took Baro and Elrin with us? Aden would grumble, but the children would love it. It might even make Baro stop crying about his ruined masterpiece. I opened my mouth to suggest it.

"And don't think you can leave me with this mess,"

Gilma said. "I won't stand for it. You're not actually of royal blood, you know. You may like to forget it, but I assure you, no one else in this castle ever does."

I shut my mouth.

Aden looked from Gilma to me. "Er . . . should I help clean up?"

"Nope," I said. I kissed Baro's smooth cheek and put him down. Glitter scattered off my skirt and rained down on the floor. "I'm sure Gilma can handle all this. Let's go."

◆

As we walked through the hallway, I felt a tiny bit guilty for leaving the children behind. But Aden's presence at my side was worth the discomfort. I hadn't seen him for two weeks. And though it wasn't unusual for him to disappear without telling me why, it still made me panic every time. I had spent the past fourteen days wondering if I had done something to make him hate me, or if someone had told him something terrible about me, or if he had just realized that nobody else in the castle understood why he spent so much time with me.

If he had finally realized I wasn't worth it.

I couldn't have blamed him if he had. When Aden wasn't around, it was glaringly obvious how much everyone else in the castle disliked me. Nobody was outright mean to me, not since Gilma's punishment after the hair incident. But they didn't meet my eyes; they spoke to me only as much as was strictly necessary; and they certainly never, ever invited me to do anything with them.

I knew I was supposed to be grateful that Gilma had been punished—like I was supposed to be grateful for everything the queen did for me. But it had made my life a million times harder. The other girls didn't dare touch me anymore, but they made up for it with sly jeers and caustic laughs, a hundred tiny cuts a day. They never let up, and they never would.

If Queen Ella had asked for my advice back then, I would have told her to leave Gilma alone. But she hadn't asked. Gilma's punishment, after all, had impressed everyone with how fair and gracious the queen was. So what if it made everything worse for me?

Everyone in the castle liked *Aden*, though. The commoners joked and laughed with him, and the nobles eagerly purchased the cupcakes he brought in from the village. He was always welcome to join any group in the castle . . . as long as he didn't drag me along.

Every once in a while he took a break from being friends with me. Every time, I was terrified that he had finally given up on me, and every time, I accepted his return gratefully. But this morning, I had come to realize that I was being selfish.

"You know," I said, and my voice caught. I cleared my throat and started again. "You don't have to be my friend."

"Of course I don't have to," Aden said. He was a few steps ahead of me, and he didn't slow down. "I like you."

"Then why have you been ignoring me?"

He hesitated—just for a second, but I knew him well enough to catch it. "I haven't been. . . ."

I rushed to catch up with him, got my feet tangled together, and caught myself against the wall. Aden turned, held out a hand as if to help me, but then dropped it to his side.

"I was feeling guilty," he muttered. "I'm sorry."

"Guilty for what?"

"For nothing," he said forcefully. "I don't have anything to feel guilty about. I just got confused." He turned away. "Come on. If we don't hurry, we'll miss the parade."

He took off at a near run.

Looking back . . . If only I had stopped him. If only I had pressed him and forced him to explain.

It probably wouldn't have made a difference. That's what I tell myself now, anyway.

But we'll never know because I didn't say anything. I was relieved to be done with that conversation. So I followed him, without the slightest idea of what a terrible mistake I was making.

2

The castle battlements were made of crumbling yellowed stone. From up here, I could catch a glimpse of the sea, gray-green waves flecked with white froth. A faint fog covered the water, so I couldn't actually see the cliffs of the Larosian peninsula, where my sisters lived in exile. But a hard, tangled knot formed in my stomach every time I glanced in that direction.

It was easier to look the other way, where a long procession of people and horses filed by, accompanied by music and cheers. This was the annual royal parade, celebrating Queen Ella's marriage to the king—and my family's downfall. It always took place three days before the annual ball, the same one at which the queen had first met the prince and left one of her glass slippers behind.

They were the two most important events of the year. Naturally, I wasn't allowed to go to either one.

The parade *was* marvelous, but we could only see a

tiny portion of it from the battlements. Once the royal float and the marching band passed beyond our view, disappearing behind the city municipal building, Aden dropped onto the stone rooftop and scowled. "I wish I was there."

I made a sympathetic noise.

"It's all my brother's fault. He distracted me when I was saddling the horses, and I fell into a mud pile."

"Ouch," I said, even though I doubted it had anything to do with Aden's brother. Like me, Aden had a tendency to trip over anything it was remotely possible to trip over—tiny pebbles, his own feet, gusts of wind. He was perfectly capable of falling into a mud pile on his own.

(Also, if he'd been in the stables, it probably hadn't been a *mud* pile.)

Aden leaned back on his elbows. "Did the queen forbid you to go to the parade again? What ridiculous reason did she make up this time?"

"She didn't forbid me," I said. "I mean, she probably would have, if I had asked her permission. But I don't feel like going to a parade that's going to remind everyone what my family did to the queen."

"Nobody's thinking about that," Aden said.

"*Every*one's thinking about it, even more than usual. You've seen the float of the wicked stepfamily." It displayed three women with green-tinged skin, dressed all in black, their plaster mouths stretched into permanent cackles. "And everyone throws rotten apples at them! It's the highlight of the parade. You know that."

Aden shifted uncomfortably. I wondered how many rotten apples *he* had thrown at the stepfamily float last year. "Yeah, but there are only two stepsisters on the float. You're not included."

This was the point in these conversations when I normally gave up. Aden was a servant who brought his wages home to his mother every night to help her pay the rent for their tiny cottage. He worked overtime selling cupcakes that he bought from a woman in the village, so that his mother could afford new clothes and firewood. Getting a job in the castle stables was the best thing that had ever happened to him. He thought anyone who got to live in a castle for free shouldn't complain about anything.

But as I hopped down from the battlements, Aden sniggered and said, "Could you imagine if you *were* included? They'd have to have a statue of a five-year-old on the float! Do you think people would still throw things?"

"Of course they would." Usually I liked Aden's perpetual optimism, but sometimes it was irritating. "People hate my family. And I'm part of that family, whether a statue of me is on the float or not."

"But you're not *really*." In general, the less Aden knew

about something, the fiercer and more argumentative he got. "You didn't do anything to *Cinderella*. I mean, you probably called her that, but only because you were copying your mother and sisters. You never tried to hurt her. Or maybe you did, because you were five, but it's not like you could have done anything to her. Because of your being five."

"Do me a favor," I said. "Never try to defend me in public, okay?"

"Look," Aden said, with the air of someone reaching firm ground at last. "*You* didn't lock her into her room or forbid her to go to the ball. You didn't try to trick the king into marrying you."

"Ew," I muttered.

"And you never tried on her glass slipper! So basically, in the end, all you—" Aden stopped short. He looked at my face, as if it were doing something odd. Which, I suppose, it was. "What?"

"What?" I asked defensively.

"What!"

"Aden, I no longer have any idea what we're talking about."

Aden grinned. "You *did* try on the slipper! How is that possible? The queen is the only person whose feet can fit into them!"

"Shhh," I hissed, glancing around.

I had very few recollections of my life with my original, wicked family. Most of those memories were vague and confused, and I couldn't always tell if they were real or if they came from stories other people told about me. But I had one very clear image in my mind: my small chubby foot sliding into a sparkling glass slipper. A whisper: *They're perfect for you.* And my own pure childish delight, because I had made my mother proud of me. It had filled me with a warm, soft feeling, like the air inflating my chest was fizzy and sweet.

"The slipper fit me when I was younger," I said. And something—whether it was the way Aden's eyes widened or the memory of my mother's delighted laugh—made me add, "My feet haven't grown since then."

"Yeah, I'm sure that's true."

"It is." I slipped off my shoe and held out my foot, wiggling my toes. My stocking had a hole in it, so my big toe stuck out. Purple glitter was scattered on my toenail.

"Wow," Aden said. "Your feet are *freakishly* small."

There was nothing freakish about it. Tiny feet were dainty and beautiful—everyone knew that. Adult women with small feet wore elaborate footgear to draw attention to them, and those unfortunate enough to have large feet made sure to wear skirts long enough to hide them. There was no such thing as too-small feet.

"And they *smell!*" Aden said, waving his hand in front of his face. "Anyhow, your feet might be weirdly small, but they're not as tiny as the queen's. There's no way you could fit into her shoes."

I knew what he was doing. But I couldn't help myself. Aden was very good at getting people to do what he wanted. (Usually, what he wanted was for them to pay ridiculous prices for his cupcakes, but sometimes he had darker designs.) "Yes, I could."

"Want to bet? I saw the queen on her way to the parade. She wasn't wearing the glass slippers."

Of course she wasn't. Queen Ella wore the glass slippers only once a year at the annual ball, which was still three days away. The rest of the time, she kept them in a locked box at the very back of her closet.

"Forget it," I told Aden. "I'm not that stupid."

Aden snorted. "Not that brave, you mean." He got to his feet. "I have to go, anyhow. When people get back from the parade, they're going to be hungry, and I convinced Dame Yaffa to make almond cupcakes this week."

"Good luck." Not that he needed luck. People went crazy for those cupcakes. "Do you have any to spare?"

"I'll give you what I have left over," Aden said, like he always did.

I made a face at him. No cupcakes were ever left over. "I'm going to rescue the princes from Gilma."

And that was what I meant to do. *Really*.

But his dare settled like an itch under my skin. The way back to the nursery *did* pass the queen's room, and the queen's door was open. . . .

And the slippers were not safely packed away in their box. They were side by side on the foot of the queen's canopy bed.

I stopped in the doorway. The sun hit the slippers with a burst of light, and brilliant sparkles danced across them, making them glitter with subtle rainbow colors. The itch went deeper, digging into my bones, making my whole body tense. It felt like something important was about to happen.

They're perfect for you.

Was it a real memory? The warmth and love in my mother's voice, the slipper sliding onto my foot like it belonged there. The softness of her hands stroking my hair, her chest rumbling against my cheek as she laughed. It felt so true. But how could it be, when everyone knew how wicked and cruel she had been?

When Cinderella's father had married my mother, I was only a baby. It had been harder for my older sisters—already twelve and thirteen years old, suddenly saddled with a new father, and a new sister their own age. By the time I was old enough to understand, Cinderella's father had died, and my mother and three sisters were all I knew. My brief, vague memories of those times were happy.

But I didn't have that many memories.

I walked through the half-open door into the room. The slippers gleamed, as if my presence made them brighter. My muscles were so tight they hurt, and energy tingled through my body.

I shouldn't do this, I thought, but my feet kept moving. I didn't even glance back at the door before I slid my fingers against one of the slippers.

My skin sparked when I touched it, as if something fierce and wild was running through that smooth, crystalline glass. All I had to do was put it on, and that wildness would be in me.

I put it on.

It fit perfectly. It fit like it had been made for me.

No *way* did it fit Queen Ella this well.

I slid my other foot into the second slipper, and a charge went through me. All at once, I wanted to dance.

So I did.

Normally, I couldn't dance more than two steps without falling flat on my face, knocking over every vase within striking distance, or simultaneously breaking two windows (a story for another time). But with the glass slippers on my feet, I bowed and leapt, landed lightly on my tiptoes, and twirled again without even feeling dizzy. I two-stepped across the room, feeling smooth and graceful, then held my arms out wide and twirled.

Then the realization of what I was doing hit me. Of how this would look to anyone who walked past the queen's still-open door.

I pulled the slippers off with a pang. My skin still fizzed with that sense of magic, but I forced myself to put the slippers down exactly where I had found them. I lined them up carefully, parallel but not touching, toes pointing toward the door. I stepped back and examined them. They looked just as they had when I found them.

The tingling in my bones sharpened into pain. My feet twitched. I made myself turn and walk toward the door.

The hall was, fortunately, empty.

I glanced back into the room. The slippers looked abandoned and forlorn. They were meant to be danced in. They *wanted* me to dance in them.

That urgent thrill rose in me, and I stepped toward the bed. Then I heard a distant sound—a thud, or maybe a footstep.

I pivoted and ran down the long hallway in the other

direction. I didn't stop until I was near the nursery. Then I leaned against the wall while my breath steadied, astonished at my own daring, still shivering with the memory of those slippers on my feet.

But mostly, I was vastly relieved that nobody would ever find out what I had done.

3

"I didn't do it," I said.

My voice shook, which made it sound like I was lying. I heard it, but I couldn't fix it. It was all I could manage not to burst into tears right there in the throne room.

Besides, it didn't matter what my voice sounded like. Not a single person in the castle—not a single person in the *kingdom*—was going to believe me.

The queen sighed.

Queen Ella sat on her throne, dressed in a long, shimmering gown of white and silver. Next to her, the king's throne was empty, and so was the rest of the room. Even the servant who had come to summon me had left, though he was probably eavesdropping outside the door.

The emptiness, the queen had explained, was a kindness. She was giving me a chance to confess, and to tell her where her slippers were, before she was forced to tell everyone I had stolen them.

She was so certain I was guilty. It was enough to make me wonder if maybe I *had* stolen the slippers and somehow forgotten about it.

"I promise!" I said. My voice came out thin and shrill. Even *I* wouldn't have believed me.

Queen Ella rose. Her gown fell in graceful folds around her as she stepped down from the dais. She stood a bit too close for comfort, towering over me.

My knees started dipping outward into an instinctive curtsy. I forced them to snap straight. I had curtsied once when I entered the throne room, like I was supposed to. I wasn't going to *grovel*.

I stared at my feet—clad in clunky outdoor shoes, because I'd gone looking for Aden after the parade ended—and at the delicate satin shoes peeping out from under the queen's lace-trimmed hem.

"Tirza," Queen Ella said. Her voice was kind, but with an edge to it. Nobody but me ever seemed to hear that edge. "Look at me."

Queen Ella's face was grave but beautiful. Her golden hair was coiled into intricate braids and held back from her face by a thin silver crown. Her eyes were soft and brown and full of disappointment.

"I understand why you did it," she said. "I know life

in this castle can be difficult for you. There are people here who haven't forgotten what your mother and sisters did to me. Some of them even believe you must be like my other stepsisters. I wish I could make things easier for you."

Her voice was so gentle. But I heard clearly the sentence she wasn't saying: *And I can make them much harder for you.*

"Just tell me where the slippers are," Queen Ella said. "We'll put them back where they belong. In three nights, I'll wear them at the ball, just like I always do. Nobody else has to know that you took them."

Tears sprang to my eyes. I knew that if I blinked, they would spill down my cheeks, and I could *not* allow that. In the six years I had been living in this castle, I had never let anyone see me cry.

So I opened my eyes very wide. The tears that filled them blurred my vision, turning the queen's face into a smudge of gold and white with two hard pinpoints of brown.

I was sure she could see guilt written all over my face. I should never have tried on those slippers. I should never have danced in them.

I should never have wanted them.

Queen Ella ended the silence with a sigh. Her features fell into lines of fierce, haughty pride—the expression I hated the most, and the one that always seemed to bode the worst for me. As if she was reminding herself that she was a queen now, and I was nothing.

"I had hoped we could manage this on our own," she said. "But now, I'm afraid, it will be necessary to get the king involved. Wait here."

She circled me, gliding gracefully. Her footsteps slid along the marble floor, then faded away.

Finally, I let the tears flow over my face. They tasted hot and salty, and I dabbed at them angrily with my sleeves. Unfortunately, my sleeves were still muddy from when I'd fallen on my way back to the castle.

Sunlight streamed in through the large windows, making the unlit chandeliers glitter. The two thrones on the raised dais gleamed so bright they almost blinded me. I had never spent much time in the throne room—the queen clearly didn't want me there. But I loved how beautiful and spacious it was, how airy and elegant.

Now the space around me felt vast and terrifying, and the light was harsh and unforgiving.

"I didn't do it," I whispered to the empty room, trying to make my voice convincing. A heaviness rose in my chest, and I found myself shouting, "I *didn't*!"

Even with no one listening, I sounded guilty. The sun glinted off the thrones and danced hot and accusing across my face.

It knew as well as I did that no one was going to believe me.

———◆———

It took nearly an hour for the king to arrive.

By the time he did, I had myself mostly under control. I'd ended up crying a little bit more—I couldn't help it—but I was done with that now. I scrubbed my face dry with a nonmuddy portion of my sleeve as King Ciaran walked in with his entourage behind him.

He must have just finished meeting with his council, because they were all there: the commander of the guard in the fake armor he wore at court, the tax collector in his red-trimmed robes, and even the spymaster with his dour expression. The minstrel was there, too, her eyes gleaming with excitement—she had hated me ever since the time she sang her *Stepsisters* ballad at court, and the queen forced her to take out the lines, "our queen took the daughter of wickedness within her arms, heedless of the inevitable harm."

(Honestly, if the queen hadn't been so outraged, nobody would have focused on those lines long enough to figure out what they meant. Eventually, the minstrel— who rewrote her ballads entirely whenever she was struck by inspiration—would have come up with some new verses that actually rhymed. But ever since Queen

Ella had made such a big deal about it, that stanza had become a popular ditty. The castle children played jump rope to it.)

The king and queen ascended the dais together, then turned in sync and sat on their thrones. The king was tall and broad, with black hair; beside him, Queen Ella looked tiny and delicate, glimmering in silver and white. They moved in perfect unison, and before they turned to glare down at me, they exchanged a wordless glance that seemed like an entire private conversation.

Together with the king's guards and the castle seneschal and a few curious nobles, about twenty people stood in the throne room.

"Tirza," the king said coldly.

"Your Majesty," I replied, and curtsied.

"I was meeting with my council on a matter of utmost importance," King Ciaran said. "Glenallan's army has been encroaching into our eastern border. Dozens of villages are in jeopardy. Yet I find myself called away to deal with . . . *this*."

King Ciaran never even pretended to like me. He was usually disdainful and remote, like he was trying to forget I existed.

I strongly preferred that to the times when he actually focused on me.

The king had a fierce, proud face, with cheekbones

that jutted out beneath his dark eyes. Everything about his expression and his bearing was regal and proper, but his hair was always the slightest bit unkempt over his forehead, a few strands straggling over the gold band he usually wore. I suspected he did that on purpose, to make himself look less grim. It didn't work.

"It's not enough," the king went on, "that every kingdom on our border will try to conquer ours the moment we show weakness. It seems we must also deal with attacks from within our own home."

With the king glowering at me and everyone else taking their cue from him, I couldn't manage to say, *I didn't do it.*

"My wife's glass slippers"—the king turned a warm, loving smile on Queen Ella, then switched instantaneously back to icy coldness when he looked at me— "are what brought us together. They are proof of our queen's fae heritage. To steal them is not just the act of a spiteful, ungrateful girl. It is *treason.*"

A horrified murmur swept through the throne room. I heard a tiny squeak, like that of a trapped mouse, and realized that I had made it.

The punishment for treason was death.

Everything the king said about the slippers was true. Before the ball where the king and queen met, it had been decades since magic had touched the royal family.

King Ciaran's great-grandmother had been able to heal mortal wounds, and *her* great-grandfather had occasionally managed to turn objects to gold, and *his* grandmother had magical hair ... and *her* great-grandmother, so it was said, was one of the faeries. Fae magic ran in the blood of the royal family, even stronger than it did in the common people. At least, it was supposed to. But it had been three generations since a king or queen of Tarel had shown an affinity for magic.

Queen Ella might have been a commoner by birth, but the fact that she could wear faerie slippers proved that she had faerie blood. She might bring magic back into the royal line. When you combined her beauty and her kindness with her faerie blood, she was the most beloved queen the kingdom of Tarel had ever had. Everyone loved her. Everyone wanted to protect her from those who would hurt her.

"I didn't ...," I tried. My voice was so quiet that even the whispering from the nobles drowned it out. "I ... I ..."

"I believed you were different," Queen Ella said, and the whispering stopped. "You were only a child when your mother and sisters were so cruel to me. Everyone advised me to send my third stepsister into exile along with the other two. But I'd hoped you were too young to have absorbed their hatred. I wanted you to have a chance. I raised you in my castle, as if you were my own daughter."

That was an exaggeration. I was pretty sure people didn't stick their *own* daughters in the most out-of-the-way, mice-infested room in the castle. People didn't forbid their own daughters from going to any balls or parades. They didn't allow the court to talk about them in a constant undercurrent of snide whispers.

Of course, the worst thing I could do would be to say any of that right now. I knew the rules: I had to be grateful to the queen, always and forever, because she had forgiven me for my family's crimes.

So I swallowed my rage. But it burned deep in my gut, and somehow made me able to breathe again.

"I didn't do it," I said. My voice was far too loud and high-pitched, but at least it didn't shake. "You're assuming I did it for no reason except who I am. I've never stolen anything from anyone, and I definitely did not steal your glass slippers!"

I managed not to end with a shout. My last words rang clear in the suddenly silent throne room.

"My dear," Queen Ella said. "Of course we would never accuse you based on nothing but assumptions. I *know* you stole the slippers." She pulled her hand from the king's grasp. "I know you did it, Tirza, because I saw you do it."

4

The court erupted in gasps and exclamations. More people drifted in through the open doors of the throne room to see what was going on.

"No," I said. "That's not true." But nobody heard me.

Queen Ella clapped her hands, and everyone went silent.

"This morning," she said, "when most of us were at the parade, I was feeling unwell. I went back to the castle."

The throne room swam around me. I thought I might faint.

"When I reached my bedroom," the queen went on, "I saw you pick up my glass slippers and put them on your feet."

This time I couldn't say "I didn't do it." Even now, with the whole court staring at me, I remembered how the slippers had felt in my hands, cool and smooth and inviting.

I should have put them down and left the room. If only I had. If only I could go back in time and tell my stupid self from this morning to just *put the slippers back on the bed.*

Instead, I had danced around the queen's room in them, leaping and twirling. And Queen Ella had been watching the entire time?

"I'm sorry," I said, my face burning. "I know I shouldn't have. But . . . if you were watching, you know I didn't take them. I put them back on your bed! You saw that, right?"

Even I heard how pathetic I sounded. Such an *obvious* lie.

I stared desperately at the queen. Queen Ella *had* always been kind to me, at least outwardly. She didn't want to hurt me. Not really.

"I shouldn't have picked them up," I said. "But they were sitting there on your bed, and they felt . . . it seemed like . . ."

"Don't be ridiculous," the queen said. "They were not on my bed. They were in the box at the bottom of my closet, as they always are. And the box was locked. How did you open it?"

"I didn't," I said. "That's not where they were."

"Don't lie," the king said. His voice was extra-sharp, with something more than his usual disdain for me, but I had no idea what it was. Except that it wasn't a good sign. "You've hurt my wife enough without lying to her face. She wept in my arms after she realized what you had done to her."

"I was so shocked." The queen's eyes welled up. She dabbed at them delicately with the lace at the end of her sleeve. "I left at once to find Ciaran and ask him what to do. Then I thought better of it and decided to talk to you myself. I went back to the room. But by then you were gone, and so"—Queen Ella's voice caught on a sob—"so were my slippers."

"I put them back," I said. "Back on the bed, exactly where they were when I found them. And then I left. I promise!"

"So you claim," the king said, "that someone came into the room in the few minutes between when you left and the queen returned, and *that* person took the slippers?" He waited, as if expecting me to say something— I had, of course, nothing to say—then shook his head. "Take her away."

"To her room," the queen put in.

One of the guards pushed between the nobles at the door, dipped in the briefest bow to the king and queen, and strode over to me. Before he could reach me, the minstrel stepped in his way.

"I'll take the child," she said. Her hand closed around my wrist, far more tightly than necessary, and she pulled me across the room. A noblewoman swept her skirt out of the way, and the seneschal stepped back ostentatiously so I wouldn't touch him.

"A guard should take her," the court scribe said. (He and the minstrel had never gotten along. Apparently, her songs weren't "historically accurate," and apparently, his reports were "so boring no one cared if they were true or not.") "And shouldn't the girl be in chains?"

"That won't be necessary," the minstrel said. "I think I can handle one eleven-year-old child."

"Don't forget where she comes from," the scribe snapped. "There is wickedness in her blood. See to it that she does not escape."

"Don't worry yourself," the minstrel said. "Even if she managed to get away from me, where would she escape *to?*"

In the even deeper silence that followed that question, she turned and led me out of the throne room.

◆

My room was in the southwest tower, which was the narrowest tower in the castle and the farthest from the throne room. It was a long way to walk in silence.

But silence was better than the alternative. The minstrel was humming under her breath, which meant she was composing a new ballad in her head. I didn't want to hear it.

So I walked as fast as I could, forcing her to keep up with me instead of the other way around. The minstrel was wearing one of her signature "waterfall dresses," with a skirt that spread out from her hips and then fell to the floor. It was held up with heavy steel wires, which meant that as long as I walked swiftly, she would be too out of breath to start singing to me.

I hoped.

It mostly worked. Even though I tripped and stumbled twice, I was able to keep up the pace. Once we reached the tower, we climbed a narrow, slightly wobbly set of stairs to the landing outside my room, and the minstrel's breath came in huffs. I opened my door and darted inside before she could have the satisfaction of pushing me in.

She had let go of my wrist, probably because she needed to support herself against the doorframe. I walked to my bed and sat with my back to her.

"I always knew this would happen," the minstrel said in a tone of great satisfaction. "It's so tragic and so inevitable. It will make a *marvelous* ballad. People will weep over your story for centuries."

"That sounds fun," I muttered. Not that I was worried; the minstrel couldn't make a *marvelous ballad* out of a successful dragon hunt or a doomed love story. She was way too fond of flowery language (one stanza of *The Wicked Stepsisters* was composed entirely of adjectives), and she played fast and loose with the concept of rhyming. Then again, she would be singing to a very receptive audience, so who knew? Maybe this *would* be the ballad that made her famous enough to get a post in a richer kingdom than ours.

Which would at least be a silver lining.

"What rhymes with *guilty*?" the minstrel mused out loud. "*Quilty*? *Wilty*? 'She could not deny that she was guilty; her voice trembled, all soft and lilty. . . .'"

"I *do* deny that I'm guilty," I snapped. "Why don't you try finding a rhyme for *innocent*?"

The minstrel made an impatient motion with her hand. "Nothing rhymes with *innocent*."

"Nothing rhymes with *guilty* either. Those aren't real words!"

"I will not be bound by the conventions of language," the minstrel said airily.

"Or by the conventions of truth? Because I *am* innocent. I didn't do it."

The minstrel's fingers twitched, as if she was reaching for a quill. "If you're to have any hope of being forgiven, Tirza, you need to return the slippers to the queen in time for her to wear them at the ball. So you have to confess within the next two days. You might as well do it to me. I will bring the news to the court and frame it as kindly as I can. I will soften it with song." She pursed her lips. "Chess."

"What?"

"*Chess* rhymes with *confess*. 'She was like a pawn in a game of chess....'"

"That doesn't even make sense! And *dress* also rhymes with— Never mind," I said as the minstrel's eyes brightened. "Just go away."

"The longer you wait, the worse it will be for you. When the king said 'Take her away,' he didn't mean to your room. You know that, right?"

"I didn't do it," I said again. Not because I thought she, of all people, would believe me. She was too delighted with the story she was already spinning in her mind. But *not* saying it felt like admitting defeat.

"Please." The minstrel arched an eyebrow. "Everyone knows that your family has always desired those slippers. Your sisters cut their own toes off to fit into them."

"They did not!" I said. "That never happened."

Her eyes glittered. Of course she believed that ridiculous story about my sisters; she had already written three stanzas about it. "The only question is why it took you so long. Why *now*, Tirza? Right before the ball? Did Dame Yaffa put you up to it?"

I blinked. Dame Yaffa was the village woman who baked the cupcakes Aden sold in the castle. Apparently, she'd had some feud with the queen in the past, so he had to do it secretly. I'd always loved the fact that there was something going on in the castle that I knew about and Queen Ella didn't . . . but maybe I hadn't understood what was going on after all. "I've never met Dame Yaffa."

"Your lies get less and less believable, child. Everyone knows Dame Yaffa was your mother's best friend."

I flinched. "Everyone except me. I was only five years old when my mother died."

The minstrel pursed her lips. "Do you truly expect me to believe Dame Yaffa never contacted you? A woman with that much fae blood could certainly have found a way to—"

Footsteps clattered on the stairs, and she went silent. A guard appeared behind her. My view of him was mostly blocked by the minstrel's voluminous skirt and draping sleeves, but the sound of his clinking sword was unmistakable.

"I'm here to guard the prisoner," he said. He sounded out of breath.

I had never realized the stairs to my room were so difficult for adults. It was pretty rare that anyone bothered to climb them. Usually, only the queen came to visit me, and *she* was never out of breath. Though if the stories were true, she had pretty good stamina.

Or maybe she was just never in a rush when she came to see me.

"Of course," the minstrel said, and stepped backward. The guard moved hastily out of the way of her skirt. "I hope you consider what we discussed, child. If you tell me the truth, I can help you."

"I *did* tell the truth," I said.

The guard laughed. He waited for the minstrel to get her skirt out of the doorway, then slammed the door shut, leaving me alone in my room.

A moment later, I heard the click of the lock.

5

I closed my eyes and flopped backward onto my bed, trying to ignore the murmuring from the other side of the door. I couldn't make out what the guard and the minstrel were saying, but they were laughing a lot, and I was pretty sure it wasn't because they were telling knock-knock jokes.

I was used to having people sneer at me. But my room, so out-of-the-way and inaccessible, was the one place where I usually didn't have to put up with it.

I loved my room—a bit defiantly, because I was pretty sure I wasn't supposed to. Queen Ella had introduced it to me as "cozy," but what that meant, apparently, was tiny and overrun with mice. You could have fit ten of this room in the queen's spacious, elegant bedchamber. But this was still a castle, so the room was beautiful despite itself. The walls were painted blue, which happened to be my favorite color, and the large curved window faced

41

east, the direction of the sea and the Larosian peninsula, where my sisters were imprisoned; the view was meant as a warning. But every morning, golden sunlight spilled over my bed, and I woke to the caws of seagulls and the crash of waves.

I tried to think. Who *had* stolen the slippers? Almost everyone in the castle had been at the parade ... but someone could have slipped back in. Maybe the true culprit had noticed me leaving the room and seen an opportunity.

But was it an opportunity to steal the slippers? Or was the true purpose to get me thrown out of the castle, cast into exile along with the rest of my family?

I rolled off the bed and paced around the room. Which was far too small for pacing, so after a few frustrating moments, I gave up and went to the window. The Larosian cliffs rose menacingly from the sea mist, gray and jagged, making my stomach twist with something barbed and painful. I tried to figure out what the feeling was—guilt? Grief? Fear?—but it wasn't quite any of those.

Everyone thought the queen was so merciful for exiling my sisters to Larosia instead of having them killed. Merciful and stupid.

Though the sisters shouldn't be much trouble, I had once overheard the kennel master say. *Lucky for the queen that her stepmother managed to get herself killed. Now we don't have to worry about that cursed family, except for—*

He had seen me then and abruptly stopped talking.

His companion, a groom, had sneered at me. "Well," he'd said, "anyone else who tries to hurt the queen, guess they'll be put on a boat to Larosia, too."

Nothing could hurt the queen more than the loss of her slippers—one of the last remaining faerie objects in existence. But who, aside from me, could possibly want to hurt the queen? Everyone loved her.

Except Dame Yaffa, apparently. But if some village woman had been near the queen's room that day, someone would have noticed. No, one of the residents of the castle must have done this. And as hard as I tried, I couldn't come up with a single suspect.

Except, of course, for me.

The sky outside my window turned dusky gray, and no one brought me dinner. I wasn't very hungry, but it didn't seem like a good sign. And when the darkness filled my window and crept into my room, no one came to light the candles in my wall sconces. It got darker and darker until I could barely see my hand when I held it up in front of my face.

I should go to bed, I thought. I would need my strength for . . . for . . .

For what?

I didn't know. I had no idea how I would be punished. I got into bed and pulled my blanket to my chin.

Vague shadows moved against the wall. Outside my door, the guard coughed.

I expected to cry myself to sleep. I tended to do my crying in bed at night. But the tears wouldn't come, maybe because I was afraid the guard would hear. I twisted and rolled over, trying to get comfortable. Outside my window, the moon had risen bright and full, and I knew that if I turned my head at the right angle, I would see the cliffs of the peninsula silhouetted against the sky.

I didn't turn my head. Not even when tears finally welled up in my eyes and ran over the sides of my face and into my ears, which was extremely uncomfortable. I rubbed my ears irritably before sliding my hands back under my blanket.

Near the wall, mice squeaked and skittered reproachfully, disappointed by my lack of dinner. Usually, I left them crumbs—and often, when dessert was particularly horrible, I left them the whole thing. I silently apologized to them as I lay in bed, staring up at the ceiling.

I must have fallen asleep eventually, because I woke with a gasp. It was still nighttime, but something had woken me. A sound.

I wasn't alone.

"Queen Ella?" I said, but I knew it wasn't her, even before I finished asking. By the moon's faint golden light,

I could make out the shape at the foot of my bed. It was much shorter and less skirted than the queen.

"Aden!" I said in relief.

Aden moved closer. Now I could see the outlines of his face, his wide cheeks and thick eyebrows.

"Tirza," he whispered. "Are you all right?"

"For now." I scrambled off the bed, glad that I had never changed into nightclothes. "How did you get in here? Did the guard leave?"

"He's still there. But he dozed off and didn't see me."

Well, at least they didn't consider me dangerous enough to give me a *competent* guard. "What are people in the castle saying?"

Aden coughed. "Um . . . you know. Stuff."

I *did* know. I resisted the urge to ask for details.

"Did you tell them?" I asked.

"Tell them what?"

"That I only tried on the slippers because you dared me to?"

He stepped back. "Don't be ridiculous, Tirza. I didn't force you to do anything."

I opened my mouth and then shut it. He was right. Much as I wanted someone to blame for this, it was entirely my own fault.

"Tirza," Aden said. "Don't be mad, but . . . *did* you take them?"

It felt like all the air had left my body. "How can you ask me that?"

"Don't yell," he hissed. "You'll wake the guard. It's just . . . Doesn't it seem a little coincidental that someone happened to steal the slippers *right* after you tried them on?"

"Yes," I agreed. "A little *too* coincidental. Almost like someone was following me, waiting for their chance."

"But the queen must have been there just a few minutes later," Aden protested. "How would anyone get in and out that fast, without either of you seeing them?"

"If you're so sure I'm guilty," I snapped, "then why did you even bother sneaking in here?"

As soon as I said it, I regretted it. Aden was the only friend I had left. (Also the only friend I'd had to begin with.) I couldn't afford to make him angry.

But Aden—who normally took offense if I so much as rolled my eyes at him—just shrugged. He was chewing the corner of his lips, the way he did when he felt guilty about something.

"I came to bring you a message," he said.

Something rustled in the corner, and we both jumped. Aden laughed shakily. "Mice again?"

The mice made Aden furious. He liked to point out that the queen would never have allowed mice to infest *her* children's nursery or the rooms where anyone of importance stayed. But they didn't *scare* him.

Why was he so jumpy?

"A message from who?" I asked.

"I think it's from someone who can help you." Aden handed me a piece of paper, folded over four times. "You're supposed to open it in private."

I took the paper. Aden shifted from one foot to another. The silence stretched, interrupted only by the skittering in the corner and an occasional squeak.

"That's it?" I asked finally.

"I brought you a cupcake too." He held out a small white box wrapped in yellow ribbon—*You can charge twice as much for a cupcake if it's in a fancy box*, he had told me once—and put it on my bed.

Aden had never given me one of his precious cupcakes before. I didn't have any money to pay him with, and he was a big believer in "not mixing business with friendship," which was a fancy way of saying "not giving stuff away for free."

Something inside my chest heaved, and I knew I was about to start crying. Again.

Aden took two steps toward the door. "I have to go before the guard wakes up."

I wondered if I should say *thank you*. I wasn't sure I could speak around the lump in my throat.

Aden was gone before I could make up my mind.

With no one there to see, I was able to contort my

face into a variety of odd expressions in an attempt to hold off tears. It worked; eventually, I pushed my tears back into my throat and then down in a burning pulse to my stomach. They coiled deep in my gut, along with my hurt and my rage.

When I had myself under control, I unfolded the paper. It was wrinkled and damp, covered with spidery words in a cramped, unfamiliar handwriting:

> We know you have the slippers.
> We're proud of you.
> You are not alone.
> It is time for us to take back what is ours.

I dropped the paper as if it had singed my fingertips, then stood perfectly still while the tears tried to get back up my throat. A sob escaped before I could control it, and I stuffed my fist into my mouth.

I bent, crumpled up the paper, and threw it as hard as I could into the corner. It bounced off the wall and across the floor, coming to rest near a scattering of mouse droppings.

It's from someone who can help you, Aden had said. But he was one hundred percent wrong. This message was from the last two people in the world who could help me now.

My sisters.

6

My clearest memory of my family was of the day they were taken away from me.

The waiting boat had been covered entirely with thick black paint, without even a name painted on its side. It didn't need one. Everyone knew what this boat was used for.

"Very subtle," my oldest sister, Danica, sneered. My sisters stood in the shadow of the boat, in chains. "I am fully convinced now that this is not a pleasure cruise. Is there anything else you need to add in order to make the point?"

Esme, my second sister, was not holding up as well. She was whimpering and looking about frantically, like she thought maybe someone was coming to save her and just running a bit late.

I stood across from them, which felt wrong. But I also didn't want to be *with* them. I didn't want chains holding my wrists together, I didn't want everyone to hate me, and I definitely did not want to get on that boat.

A hand closed around mine. Cinderella—no, it was *Queen* Ella now—smiled down at me.

You're safe, she had told me earlier that day. (Or maybe it had been later that day? My memory was fuzzy on that.) *None of this is your fault. Now that I'm queen, I can protect you.*

Her slim fingers tightened on my small hand, and I felt the dampness of her sweat in my palm. Cinderella was not as assured as she appeared.

Danica's eyes narrowed. Her gaze focused on the spot where Cinderella's hand was wrapped around mine. For the first time, her defiant mask cracked, allowing a hint of hurt through.

I yanked my hand free, and Danica turned to face Cinderella.

"You think you're a queen now?" she said. "You think people will ever look at you and see anything but a pathetic servant girl with cinders in her hair? We're your family. We were the only ones who ever might have loved you. You'll regret sending us away." Her chin wobbled and then firmed. She, too, wasn't as confident as she appeared. "And you'll regret what you did to my mother."

Esme let out a sob and covered her face with her hands. Loud snorts emerged from behind her fingers.

Cinderella took my hand again. This time, she didn't

let me pull free. She held on with bruising force, pulling me up the narrow stone stairway and into the castle.

"Take them away," she said over her shoulder.

So I never got to watch my sisters being led into the boat. Never got to say goodbye. The last thing I heard from my family was Esme's long, bitter wail.

When Cinderella finally let go of my hand, we were back inside the castle, in a long hall with flower-patterned rugs. Any sound from outside was cut off completely by the thick stone walls. Queen Ella knelt in front of me and put both hands on my shoulders. Her eyes were wet, but her voice was steady.

"Don't worry," she said. "It's not true what Danica— It's not true. I'll keep you safe, Tirza. I promise."

I nodded.

But even then, I knew better than to believe her.

Everyone knows what happened next. My sisters were deposited on the coast of the Larosian peninsula, to make their way to the interior of that dangerous country . . . or, more likely, to die in the process. I was kept in the castle, indebted to the queen for her kindness, hated and feared by everyone.

For a while, Queen Ella made a big show of being gentle with me. She had the cook prepare my favorite foods, offered to bring my friends to the castle to play with me, and invited me to her room for private breakfasts. But the rich food gave me stomachaches, I'd never had any friends, and the last thing I wanted was to talk to her about my feelings. Everyone in the castle whispered about how ungrateful I was, and eventually, her displays stopped.

Then, six years later, I proved that the people who didn't trust me—which was all the people—had been correct. I betrayed the queen by stealing her most precious possession.

And now it was my turn to be punished.

———◆———

They *did* give me breakfast—so at least they weren't going to starve me. Yet.

It was a nice breakfast too. The usual castle fare: omelet with spices, toast with jam, a warm cup of cocoa, and a plate of fruits. They had even given me dessert: a thick slice of chocolate cake, decorated with cream that probably looked much better than it tasted. The food was all laid out on a tray, and the tray was pushed into my room so swiftly that I didn't even realize what was happening until the door slammed shut again.

I had woken up dozens of times during the night, since my brain apparently thought it was *really important* that I dream of all the various ways in which I could be punished. Every time I woke, I tried yet again to figure out who might have stolen the slippers and how they had managed it and why they had done it. But if I came up with any reasonable guesses, I had forgotten them by the time I woke again.

As a result, I was so tired I couldn't even tell I was hungry—until the smells from the tray reached me. Then I dove across the room.

I didn't even bring the tray to my bed. I ate sitting cross-legged on the floor, not slowing down until every crumb was gone. (Poor mice. Once again, I had nothing left for them.) I even ate the slice of cake, which, like most of the chef's desserts, tasted like sugared sand. Inadequately sugared sand.

It was only after I had choked down the cake that I remembered Aden's cupcake.

The box was still at the foot of my bed, where I had put it last night. The frosting had melted into a spreading pinkish-gray mass. But its smell made my stomach gurgle impatiently despite the full meal I had eaten. It smelled like the perfect mixture of sweetness and butteriness. I unpeeled the wrapper.

The cupcake came apart in my hand. One half fell to the floor, frosting-side down, with a moist plop.

I stuffed the remaining half into my mouth.

It was like eating happiness. It *was* sweet and buttery, but it also had something else that I had never tasted before and couldn't identify. It felt like it was melting onto my tongue.

I closed my eyes. For a moment, I actually forgot where I was and what was going to happen to me.

I bent, scooped up the second half of the cupcake, and ate that too.

Yes, it had been on the floor, but it couldn't have been there for more than thirty seconds, and the floor had just been cleaned. . . . Well, I wasn't exactly sure when it had been cleaned, but probably someone had cleaned it *sometime* in the past week.

It was all I could do not to scrape the remnants of frosting from the floor and eat that too. But that was just a tiny bit more disgusting than the frosting was delicious. I left it for the mice.

I used the chamber pot and changed into a green silk dress that was a bit snug on me, but still comfortable. It made me look respectable, and it had a flared skirt that was good for running in. Just in case.

Then I went to the door and knocked.

I was a bit surprised when the guard opened it immediately. I had expected to have to do some begging and crying, or maybe even pretend I was sick.

"Er," I said. "Hello."

The guard crossed his arms over his chest, his face cold and unsympathetic.

Granted, when they were choosing men to be guards, *sympathetic* was probably not high on their list of desired qualities.

"I'm hungry," I said. I did my best to look piteous. "Breakfast wasn't enough for me. I've had nothing else to eat since yesterday morning."

"You have frosting on your nose," the guard said.

I swiped furiously at my nose. A bit of pink frosting came off on my finger.

I really wanted to eat it, but that would have been a bad idea. I decided to try another approach. "I need to talk to the queen. About the slippers."

The guard's eyebrows slanted downward. He eyed me, as if I were a clump of dirt that it should be someone else's job to clean up.

Then he turned and gestured for me to follow him.

It was a long walk down the stairs and through the corridors. The faces of the courtiers as I trudged through the halls were worse than the guard's.

And the faces of the king and queen, after the guard let me into the royal sitting room . . .

At least they were alone. I had been afraid they would have servants with them, and even more afraid that the princes would be there. Elrin was too young to understand any of this, but Baro knew what *stealing* meant. He knew how precious the glass slippers were.

Gilma had probably told him already. She had always hated the fact that the princes preferred me over her. But Baro never believed anything she said, not since the time she had promised having a splinter removed wouldn't hurt at all.

He believed everything his mother told him, though.

A lump rose in my throat, and it was harder to push down than usual. But I managed. I couldn't afford to break down, not now.

King Ciaran and Queen Ella sat together on an ivory-and-gold couch, sharing a tray of cinnamon pastries. They were wearing robes over their nightclothes, and the queen's hair was down and unbrushed, tumbling over her shoulders. King Ciaran was lounging back on the couch with one foot propped up on a footstool, crumbs flaking over the front of his robe. As soon as he saw me, he put his foot down and sat up straight.

I curtsied, mostly so I wouldn't have to look at their faces while I spoke. I knew what I had to say. That didn't make it any easier to say it.

I overbalanced slightly on the curtsy, stumbled forward, and straightened too fast. That didn't help either.

"Well?" the king demanded. "Why are you here?"

Heat flushed through me, and I couldn't move my mouth. The thought of saying what I had come to say, of the way their expressions would change ...

I couldn't. I *couldn't*.

You can do anything.

A memory of a voice saying that to me, a long time ago. My mother's voice, soft and fierce.

I cleared my throat and blurted out the words. That was all I had to do. Once they were out, I couldn't take them back.

"Your Majesties," I said, "I am here to confess."

Something thudded in the doorway, and we all turned as a chambermaid backed away from the door and into the hall. My heart sank. Not that it really mattered; the guard was outside the door too. He would gossip to the other guards, and they would tell the chambermaids, who would tell the ladies' maids, who would tell their ladies ... By the time I stepped out of this room, the news of my confession would be all over the castle.

So it almost didn't matter what I said next. All the same, I went on. "I saw the slippers on your bed. I put them on, and I danced in them. That was wrong. They weren't mine, and I used them without permission. I beg your forgiveness."

Queen Ella's face was perfectly still. King Ciaran leaned forward.

"And then what did you do with them?" he asked. "Where are they now?"

I lifted my chin.

"I put them back," I said. "Right back on the bed. I don't know where they are now."

The king's mouth went straight and hard. "I thought you were here to confess."

"I am," I said. "I'm confessing to what I actually did."

The king spoke through gritted teeth. "So you came here to lie to us? Again?"

"I'm not lying," I said, without bothering to put much force into it.

"You are a shameless liar and an ungrateful thief, and you should have been sent into exile with the rest of your family to begin with." He leaned back. "I've long regretted that I gave in to my bride on that point. I suppose I should thank you for giving me a reason to reverse my decision and get rid of you."

"Ciaran," Queen Ella said.

He turned on her. "I hope you can admit now that I was right. After all these years of her skulking around the castle, glaring at you, she has revealed herself to be as wicked as I always knew she was. Do you really think she deserves *more* of your kindness?"

"She's a child," Queen Ella said.

"She's not so young anymore! And even when she was,

do you remember how she attacked you? You forced me to overlook it then, but now she's ten years old—"

"Eleven." The queen and I said it simultaneously.

"Which is more than old enough to be held responsible for her actions."

I flinched. But the queen said calmly, "Let me talk to her."

"Hasn't there been enough—"

"*Alone*, Ciaran."

The king and queen looked at each other, and it was the king who looked away first.

"Indeed," he said. "So I am to leave my own sitting room, in the middle of breakfast, for the sake of this traitorous wretch?"

"Of course not." Queen Ella got to her feet, her robe falling in pale silk waves about her. "Tirza. Walk with me."

She gave me her sweetest smile and held out her hand. When I didn't take it, she sighed and let it drop. The king's scowl deepened.

A part of me preferred his honest anger to her pretense. But of course, it didn't matter what I wanted.

When the queen turned and swept out the door, I followed her.

7

The queen still had a cinnamon bun in her hand. Once we were in the hallway, she broke off half and handed it to me.

"Come," she said. "We'll go to the gardens."

I looked at the cinnamon bun with distaste. After the cupcake Aden had given me, the thought of eating one of the chef's pastries was even less appealing than usual. But refusing the bun seemed like a bad idea. So I held it in one sweaty hand, feeling glaze melt stickily against my palm as the queen led me down a back stairway and out into the castle gardens.

It was late spring, and the entrance to the garden was framed by gnarled gray vines dripping with colorful flowers. One purple petal drifted down and landed on the queen's shoulder.

From behind a delicate wrought-iron fence lined with roses, a man and woman gaped at us. They had large pouches hanging from their belts, and yellow circlets around their heads—proof that they had paid the entrance fee for the castle grounds.

The castle gardens drew visitors from throughout the twelve kingdoms—partly because of their beauty, and partly because of the famous events that had taken place here. There, beyond the rose trellis, was where the prince had asked Cinderella her name. There, on the curving staircase with the vine-wrapped railings, was the spot where Cinderella had dropped her slipper. There, in front of the endlessly tinkling fountain, was where Cinderella had confronted her stepsisters and pronounced their banishment.

I spent as little time in the gardens as possible.

The woman glanced at me, then whispered something to the man, who pulled a tattered guidebook out of his pouch and flipped through it. They weren't close enough for me to see the writing on the cover, but I recognized it by its greenish-brown color: *The Twelve Kingdoms' Best and Most Affordable Castles,* which was my least favorite guidebook. It described the queen as "a commoner more regal than any born monarch, whose generosity extends even to the potential traitor in her own home."

Queen Ella took a bite of her cinnamon bun as she turned down a curving path. "These are much better than usual," she said. Kindness oozed out of her voice, thick and smothering. Behind the fence, cloth and paper rustled as the two visitors tried to surreptitiously follow us. No doubt they would return home with tales of how gracious and kind the queen was, even to the girl who had betrayed her.

"The chef's new assistant must be better than he is," Queen Ella went on, and took another bite. "Mmm. It's really almost good."

Clearly, I was expected to respond by taking a bite myself. I had the bun halfway to my mouth when my stomach clenched. The tightness of my grip had turned the bun into a sticky mash of dough, which wouldn't have been appetizing even if my stomach hadn't been full.

I lowered my hand. I didn't *have* to take a bite. Not if I didn't want to.

Every once in a while, I engaged in these little acts of meaningless defiance.

As always, I couldn't tell whether the queen noticed. Queen Ella swept over to a bench shaped like a butterfly and gracefully lowered herself onto it.

I followed and sat as far from her as I could. It wasn't a very large bench, and the butterfly-wing decorations took up most of the sides. When I perched on the edge, the thin metal of the wings jabbed into my hip.

That often seemed to happen to me around the

queen: being forced to do something just uncomfortable enough to hurt, but not painful enough to complain about.

"I know life here hasn't always been easy for you," Queen Ella said, pretending not to notice my awkward position. "I understand why you might be angry."

The metal edge cut painfully into my skin, and I strongly suspected I was about to fall sideways off the bench. I didn't move.

"But if something is bothering you," the queen said, "you can always come talk to me. You know that, don't you, Tirza?"

I couldn't see or hear the tourists—which didn't mean they weren't listening. A yellow-and-black butterfly flitted over the bushes across the path. I wondered what it thought of the metal butterfly bench.

Queen Ella sighed into the silence. "If stealing the slippers was a cry for attention, you have succeeded. You have everyone's attention now. But, Tirza, you *must* give them back. They're dangerous."

Dangerous seemed like an odd choice of word. I glanced sideways at the queen and saw something that astonished me.

Queen Ella's lips were pressed together, her jaw clenched so tight it trembled. Her fingers dug into the silk folds of her robe.

She was *afraid*.

If I had looked a second later, I would have missed it. By the time I turned my head, the queen's face had smoothed into its usual kind, sweet expression.

I had always known that expression was just a mask. But knowing it was different from seeing it happen right in front of me.

"The thing is, Tirza," Queen Ella said, "taking the slippers was a . . . a harmless prank. We can forget all about it once you give them back."

I couldn't entirely suppress my snort. But I did manage to turn it into a sneeze. No one would *ever* forget the theft of the slippers.

It wasn't a very convincing sneeze, but Queen Ella ignored it, opening her brown eyes wide. She had ridiculously long, thick eyelashes; from this close, they looked like a cluster of little spikes protecting her eyes.

"I need to know where the slippers are," she said. "I need to dance in them at the ball. If I don't, it could be— it could be—"

Her voice trembled, the fear creeping out. She was leaning in so close that I scooted backward, right onto the point of one of the iron wings. I winced.

"*Catastrophic*," the queen finished. "For me, for you, for the entire kingdom."

"Why?" I asked.

Queen Ella's eyelashes fluttered. *"Why?"*

"Yes," I said. "Why would it be catastrophic?"

Too late, I realized that it sounded like I was admitting to stealing them.

The queen sat up. That should have been a relief, but it really, really wasn't. She eyed me with a haughty tilt of her chin, with that superior expression of hers. As if she had never been a girl named Cinderella, grubby and pathetic and covered with soot.

I remembered. I called up those memories now, as I always did when the queen tried to intimidate me: Cinderella on her hands and knees, scraping ashes into a dustpan. Cinderella dragging a bucket of soapsuds from room to room, her greasy hair plastered to her face. Cinderella lugging a basket of laundry, and a pair of knickers being tossed through the air and landing on her head. She had walked all the way to the river with the knickers *on her head.*

I remembered laughing about that. Not cruelly, of course. But it had been really, really funny.

"I didn't take them," I said.

"I've always known I can't trust anyone in this castle," the queen said. "But I thought I could trust you. You loved me once." Her spikelike lashes veiled her eyes. "You don't remember, I suppose. You were so little. When I went to the ball, you were just starting to copy your sisters, to laugh at me and order me around. But before that, I used to play with you and comfort you when you cried. The two of us were never allowed to go to parties, so we would stay home and play cards. Even though we weren't related by blood, I was your favorite sister."

"Maybe you were," I said, "before you took my family away from me."

The second the words were out of my mouth, I couldn't believe I had said them. I should have stuck to *I didn't do it.*

Judging from the expression on her face, the queen couldn't believe it either. She rose and turned, the swish of her robe hitting my legs.

"You have no chance of getting away with this, Tirza," she said. "The slippers won't allow themselves to stay hidden. One way or another, they'll make themselves known."

The sweetness was stripped from her face, revealing a hard, cold anger. Then she turned away, and I could no longer see her expression.

But I could hear the sharp edge of her voice. "Go back to your room. You have until tomorrow night to tell me where the slippers are. But if I have to go to the ball without them, there will be nothing I can do to protect you."

I did not go back to my room.

I would have to eventually, of course. I had nowhere else to go. And when I did go back, I would be in even more trouble for disobeying a direct order from the queen.

(Though really, how much more trouble could I possibly be in?)

But once I went to my room, my fate would be sealed. No one was looking for the *real* thief except me.

And now I had a clue: *It is time for us to take back what is ours.*

Aden must know *something* about where that letter had come from and what my sisters were planning.

I took off at a dead run for the stables.

———————◆———————

While I ran, I thought of several ways to convince Aden to tell me what he knew.

STRATEGY #1: beg.
Please, Aden. You're the only one I can turn to. If you won't help me, I'll be completely alone.

Ouch. The advantage was it was true. The disadvantage was, it was so true I wasn't sure I could bring myself to say it.

STRATEGY #2: threaten.
I know about the time you forgot to tie Duke Grolin's saddlebag, and about the time you accidentally let the dogs out of the kennel during Baro's birthday party, and about the time you let the horses eat the queen's picnic baskets. (There were a dozen other possibilities I could have gone with.)

The advantage was it would remind Aden of our years of loyal friendship. The disadvantage was that neither forgetting to tie a saddlebag (even if the duke's undergarments had ended up scattered all over the courtyard) nor ruining Baro's birthday—nor anything Aden had ever done, even that time he had trained a visiting baroness's horse to pull sashes off dresses—was remotely comparable to what I was accused of.

STRATEGY #3: bargain.
Help me, and I'll . . .

The disadvantage was immediately obvious: I had nothing to bargain with. The only things I owned were fancy dresses, which I suspected Aden would not be interested in. My birthday presents had always been special meals or excursions, never anything actually valuable like jewelry. Probably exactly for this reason— so I would never have anything to sell or trade if I decided to betray the queen.

And anything I could promise to *do* for Aden— help him sneak extra food from the kitchen, borrow books from the castle library, cover up his mistakes before the stable master noticed—I was already doing. There was nothing I wouldn't do for my best and only friend.

I tried to tell myself that Aden would feel the same way. That all I would have to do was ask.

But Aden had lots of people who liked him. He wasn't as desperate for my friendship as I was for his. Besides, he had always considered his problems more important than mine.

Until now, he had probably been right.

———◆———

When I got to the stables, I still hadn't decided how to approach Aden. As it turned out, that didn't matter, because Aden wasn't there. The only person in the stable was Aden's brother, Jerome, who was organizing the saddles hung on the wall.

I backed up. But I didn't notice a manure fork lying on the floor, and I tripped over it and landed on my backside in the hay. Jerome turned and stared at me.

"Should you be here?" he said. "Aren't you in prison?"

"Um," I said, scrambling to my feet.

His eyes lit up. He was holding an ornate lady's saddle decorated with pink ribbons. "Are you *escaping?*"

"No!" I said hastily.

Jerome turned and slid the saddle onto its hook. "Then why are you here? Everyone says you've been locked away while the king and queen decide whether to throw you in the dungeon or send you into exile. I bet four coppers on the dungeon."

"The queen allowed me to leave." Which was technically true. "I'm looking for Aden."

Jerome had been in the middle of bending to pick up the next saddle from the floor. He straightened and frowned at me instead. "My brother doesn't need to get mixed up in your mess. What do you want with him?"

"Where is he?" I demanded.

"Whatever you tell him, I'll beat it out of him later," Jerome warned. "He's at home."

That was a problem. I had never been to Aden's home. I was not, in fact, allowed to go to the village by myself.

But if I wandered around the castle waiting for Aden to return, it wouldn't be long before someone dragged me back to my room and locked me in. That *some*one might even be Jerome, whose expression was getting increasingly calculating.

"Excellent," I said. I tried to brush the hay off my dress. "Can you tell me how to get there?"

Jerome kicked the saddle to the side. "You wouldn't last a second on your own," he said. "I'd better show you."

I could see no way to refuse. Besides, he was probably right.

"How kind of you," I said faintly.

Jerome's smile, before he turned toward the stable doors, seemed particularly nasty. A chord of fear and distrust rang all through my body.

But what choice did I have?

"Follow me," Jerome said, and I did.

———◆———

The queen rarely took me to the village. On our last visit, she had taken me to get a dress made for Baro's birthday ball. She had helped pick out a dark green fabric, saying the color looked good on me (which was true; I still wore green whenever possible). She had let me ask for straight sleeves, even though the style at the time was for gauzy, flowing sleeves, which I hated; they tended to trail through soup and get ripped by anything with the hint of a point. She even said she would get *her* next gown made with straight sleeves, so the court would follow suit and the style would change.

It was one of the best days of my life. But then, the day before the ball, the queen decreed that I could not go.

There had been some sort of excuse, but I barely remembered it. I had thrown the green dress at the queen, and her face had gone cold and forbidding as she swept out of the room. Later, a maid had folded the dress and put it at the bottom of my clothes chest, where it had remained ever since.

Since then, all my clothes were made by the castle seamstress, even though she managed to stick me at least a dozen times during every fitting. The queen always pretended to believe it was by accident.

But that had come afterward. I forced myself to reach back through the bitter memories to the happy ones. The queen and I had ridden down in the royal coach, so I had seen the village mostly through the coach's square window—small huts and dirt streets and women hanging clothes up to dry—with my view blocked periodically by one of the guards trotting beside us. I hadn't had too long to look, because it had been only a few minutes before we arrived at the seamstress's shop.

This time there was no coach. And walking, I soon discovered, took *much* longer.

Jerome kept up a rapid pace, so I had to half jog to keep up with him. By the time we reached the main street of the village, sweat was dripping from my hair and trickling down my neck.

Jerome turned off the dirt street onto an uphill path that wound between several stone cottages. A few children playing ball stopped and stared as we went by.

A woman trudged down the path toward us, carrying a basket of laundry. Jerome walked around her, but as I followed, the woman reached out and grabbed my arm.

"I recognize you," she said.

My heart sank. She was the seamstress who had sewn the never-worn green dress.

"You're the one," she said, "who stole the queen's magic slippers."

The children's heads all whipped around. Their ball bounced down the path and rolled into the mud. One of the younger girls went after it.

The seamstress's fingernails dug painfully into my skin. "What are you doing here?"

I looked frantically for Jerome, but he had disappeared.

"If you're trying to sell the slippers," the seamstress

said, "you'll find no takers here. The queen was one of us, and she still takes care of us. We all love her."

"No! I'm not trying to sell the slippers. I mean, I don't have the slippers. I never did." I tried to pull free. The seamstress's grip tightened painfully, each of her fingers like a tiny pair of iron pincers.

I attempted to sound firm. "Let go of me at once."

The seamstress laughed.

The girl came back up the path with the ball. A group of boys about Jerome's age gathered around her. I recognized some of them—many of the villagers worked in the castle—but I'd never had much to do with them, and I couldn't remember any of their names.

"What's this I hear?" said the tallest of the boys. "Did we catch a traitor trying to escape?"

The seamstress let go of my arm, but by then, it was too late to run. The boys surrounded me.

"We should bring her back to the castle," the seamstress said.

"Oh," said one of the boys, "we will."

"Without harming her," the seamstress added. The worry in her voice made fear spike through me. "You know she is under the queen's protection."

"*Still?*" the tallest boy said. "I doubt that."

Another boy laughed. "The queen sees the truth about her now."

"Probably regrets ever taking her in."

"Should have punished her to begin with."

"We can help fix that mistake."

Prickles ran through my feet and up my legs, sharp and painful. I had never realized that fear started in your feet.

"She would deserve it," the seamstress said, addressing herself to the tallest boy. "But the queen has a strange fondness for this wicked child. If you harm her, you'll be the one who ends up punished. Remember what happened to that nursemaid?"

The boy scoffed and stepped closer. But some of the other boys hesitated.

"What's she doing here, anyhow?" one of them said. "With no guard and no escort? I bet she's trying to run away."

"Of course she's running away," another exclaimed. "She's a thief and she got caught!"

"No!" I said. It came out as a squeak. I tried again, and my voice emerged wavering but clear. "I'm not trying to run away. I'm trying to find the true thief."

"And you think you'll find a thief *here*?" another boy said. "Among us?"

"No! I need to talk to—"

I stopped. I couldn't bring Aden into this. He had to *live* here, in this village, with these boys. He didn't have any royal protection. What would they do to him if they thought he was helping me?

But what would they do to *me* if I couldn't explain why I was here?

"Well?" the girl jeered. She was younger than the boys and had been hanging back until now. The fact that she was joining in was definitely a bad sign. "Who were you going to meet?"

The seamstress stepped farther away—far enough that she wouldn't get hurt once the beating started. This, too, was a bad sign.

"No one," I said. "I'm not here to see anyone."

My voice was almost inaudible, but it didn't matter. They weren't listening for my answer. The tall boy stepped closer to me—so close I was forced to step back. I tripped and sat down hard on the dirt ground. A laugh rose all around, and the boy loomed over me, grinning with anticipation.

A tingle ran along my skin. This one also started in my feet, but it didn't feel like fear—it felt oddly familiar, a spark of power. It was what I had felt when I had the glass slippers on my feet, twirling around the queen's room.

It was so intense that for a moment, it felt more important than the beating I was about to get. I tried to look around to see what was causing it, but the tall boy scuffed a cloud of dirt at my face. I jerked my head away and covered my eyes.

"Actually," someone said from behind me, "I believe she came to speak to me."

9

The tall boy froze. I scrambled to my feet and turned. Jerome and Aden stood at the top of the path. Between them, holding each of them by an ear, was a short woman in colorful clothing.

"Come with me, child," the woman said.

She was wearing a voluminous dress of stitched-together fabrics, decorated with the oddest assortment of items—a patch of feathers, a collection of white sequins, a hodgepodge of buttons, and fragments of lace. She was so short that the hem of the dress swept the dirt, and Jerome had had to bend down to allow her to grasp his ear.

She looked ridiculous.

But the tall boy took several steps back from me, and the others shuffled their feet.

Whatever I had felt was gone. An uncomfortable

prickle ran along my skin; the remnants of a power that had fizzled into nothing.

"She's a thief!" the tall boy blurted out. But he said it like someone making excuses he knew no one would accept. "It's true, Dame Yaffa. She betrayed our queen."

Dame Yaffa? She *looked* like a baker—there was something kind and plump about her, and actually, maybe that white on her hem was flour, not lace. And there was also something familiar about her. Or was I imagining that?

Everyone knows Dame Yaffa was your mother's best friend, the minstrel had said. But I could barely remember my mother, much less her friends.

"Yes," Dame Yaffa said. "I heard about what she did." She fixed her eyes on me. They were unremarkable eyes in a round, unremarkable face. There was nothing in them to explain why all the boys were sidling away from her.

A woman with that much fae blood, the minstrel had said.

"I will deal with this," Dame Yaffa said. "Tirza, come with me."

I tried to meet Aden's gaze. Before I could, Dame Yaffa turned around and then yanked on his and Jerome's ears. They shuffled in a hasty circle around her until they were all facing the other way.

"We'll get you later," the tall boy muttered.

Dame Yaffa marched up the path, and I brushed the dirt off my face and ran to catch up.

———◆———

At the top of the hill, the path narrowed into a muddy trail. We followed it between scraggly bushes and marshy hollows. Dame Yaffa strode ahead with Jerome and Aden scurrying at her sides.

The trail led to a handful of wooden houses perched at the edge of the forest. These houses, unlike the small but neat cottages in the village, were in various states of decay: peeling paint, shutters hanging crooked, mold growing on sagging rooftops. The entire doorway of one house had no door, and a cluster of mangy dogs watched us from the front porch of another.

The last of the houses, though, was freshly painted, with gaudy flower-patterned curtains hanging in the windows. Dame Yaffa led us to the front door, which was red with bright blue trimmings.

"You had better come in," she said, and let go of the boys' ears before entering the house. Both Aden and Jerome, in identical motions, rubbed their ears and gave me reproachful looks. Like somehow this was *my* fault.

I followed them inside, still too shaky to consider any other option. Even though none of the villagers had followed us, I let out a breath of relief when the door closed behind me.

The front room of the house was the kitchen, small and spare—a stove, a butter churn, a round wooden table. Through the door at the end, I could see the common room, which in a home this size was probably also the bedroom. At night, everyone would unfold their beds and lie down to sleep, and in the morning, they would stow them away.

How do I know that? For some reason, a deep sadness welled up in my stomach.

"Sit," Dame Yaffa said. "Do you want a cupcake?"

I sat gingerly on one of the wooden chairs. "No, thank you."

She raised her eyebrows.

"I'm not hungry," I explained.

"What does that matter?" Aden asked. "It's a cupcake!"

Why, on one of the worst days of my life, did everyone insist on forcing sweets on me? Did they think a cinnamon bun, or a cupcake, were going to make anything better?

Although come to think of it, the last cupcake I'd eaten *had* made me feel better. At least while I was eating it.

"Just take one," Jerome said. "No one turns down Dame Yaffa's cupcakes."

I pressed my lips together, my feelings tangling into a knot of anger and stubbornness. For a moment, I was willing to fight *to the death* over my right to refuse this cupcake.

Then the moment passed, as it always did. Stubbornness never got me anywhere, not when I had no power to back it up with.

"Sure," I said. "Thank you."

But when Dame Yaffa produced a vanilla cupcake with pink frosting and slid it onto the table, I didn't touch it. Instead, I said, "Why are you helping me?"

"I didn't say I *was*."

Aden rolled his eyes (keeping carefully out of Dame Yaffa's sight) and gave me a crooked, encouraging smile.

I tried to feel encouraged. "Then why did you save me from those villagers?"

Dame Yaffa raised her eyebrows. "I don't think you deserve to be beaten for taking the queen's slippers. Someone should have stolen them long ago."

Oh. So it wasn't like she thought I was *innocent*.

"The queen is letting their power go to waste." Dame Yaffa sat on the chair across from me. "But I can help you learn how to use them."

"So . . . you do plan to help me?" I asked.

"Of course. I am your godmother, after all."

"My what?"

"Do you not remember me?"

I shook my head.

Dame Yaffa sighed. "I was godmother to all your sisters. I was good friends with your mother. You lived next door."

In the house now occupied by stray dogs.

That was why this house seemed familiar. That was why it made me feel sad. Because once, I had lived in a house just like it.

I burst into tears.

I wasn't expecting it, so I had no chance to guard against it. The tears came in a mad rush.

"Boys," Dame Yaffa said, "go outside."

They obeyed with immediate and obvious relief.

Dame Yaffa leaned forward. I wasn't sure if she was going to put her arms around me, and I also wasn't sure if I wanted her to. But all she did was rest her elbows on the table's rough wooden surface and watch me.

I wished she would look away.

I tried to get myself under control—to at least weep silently and with dignity, instead of in great hacking sobs that turned into uneven hiccups and sent snot, as well as tears, pouring down my face. But I couldn't. I kept weeping and hacking until finally, my body seemed to run out of tears. I gave a final honking sniffle and used my sleeve to wipe my face. (Not for the first time, so my sleeve was soaked and useless. But at least I managed to sort of even out the wetness on my face.)

The entire time, Dame Yaffa's sympathetic expression didn't change. She also didn't say anything.

The silence stretched, and finally I realized that *I* was supposed to say something. I picked up the cupcake, just so I would have something to do with my hands, and said, "I'm sorry."

"For what?" Dame Yaffa asked.

"For, um . . . for that. And for making you bring me here . . ."

"You're apologizing for crying? And for almost getting beaten up?"

Dame Yaffa clearly thought she was being kind, but all she was doing was making me want to apologize for apologizing. "I guess not?"

Dame Yaffa tilted her head to the side. "But you're not apologizing for stealing the queen's slippers?"

I hesitated. Clearly, Dame Yaffa—my godmother— thought stealing the slippers was a good thing. She thought I knew where they were and that I could "learn how to use them." That was part of the reason she was helping me. Maybe it was the whole reason.

"No," I said. "I'm not apologizing for that."

"Nor should you." Dame Yaffa pursed her lips. "It was a brilliant move. None of us thought you had it in you."

"None of *who*—"

"Those slippers are central to the legend the queen has created about herself. They're the proof that she has faerie blood." Dame Yaffa smiled thinly. "Without them, she'll no longer seem like a magical princess, so sweet and pure that she attracted the attention of the prince without even trying. People will see her for what she is—a common girl who managed to scheme her way into power."

I had never, *ever* heard anyone speak of Queen Ella with such scorn. Weirdly, it made me bristle.

"If I were you," Dame Yaffa went on, "I would have waited until the night of the ball to steal them. But I suppose you had to take your chance where you could find it." Her eyes narrowed. "How much do you remember, Tirza, about the night Cinderella stole the slippers?"

Stole?

"Not much," I admitted. "I remember"—I barely dared say it out loud—"that my mother put the slippers on me."

My heart beat frantically, as if trying to stop me. But Dame Yaffa just waited.

"And then . . . the queen stole them?" Despite Dame Yaffa's encouraging nod, it was hard to get the words out. I had never dared question the story everyone believed, not even in my own mind.

Dame Yaffa's face settled into grim lines. "Those slippers were passed down through my family for generations—one of the last faerie artifacts left in the world. Your mother was my dearest friend, and I always meant to give the slippers to one of her daughters. One of her *real* daughters." Her face softened. "Your mother tried them on you when you were a child. They fit perfectly. *You* were the one meant to wear them, not that thief who sits on the throne."

I put the cupcake down. "Then what—what happened?"

She leaned back, her gaze steady. "Do you remember how your mother died?"

The front door slammed open with a thud that made the cottage shake. Aden and Jerome pounded into the room. Right on their heels came one of the boys from the village.

The village boy stopped near the door and gave me a somewhat sheepish look, while Aden and Jerome skidded to a halt near the table.

"Royal guards," Jerome gasped. "Coming into the village. They say they're here for the thief."

10

Dame Yaffa got to her feet, her face calm. "Do the guards know Tirza is here?"

"Um." Aden rolled his eyes. "I think those boys might *tell them.*"

"I wouldn't be so sure of that," Dame Yaffa said, with steel in her voice.

"They're offering gold coins in return for information about her," Jerome said.

There was a pause.

"Right," Dame Yaffa said. "So we can hide her, or we can run, or—"

"Or," Jerome said, "we can hand her over and get those coins for ourselves."

Dame Yaffa fixed her gaze on him. Jerome scowled. "Come *on!* Don't look at me like I'm the only one who thought of it."

"I thought of it," the village boy offered.

Aden slid sideways along the wall, lifted a corner of a red-and-orange curtain, and peered out the window. "There are guards outside. But they're standing around like they're waiting for something. One of them just scratched his backside."

"Thank you," Jerome said. "Be sure to keep updating us with important information like that."

Aden dropped the curtain and stepped back. "We have to get Tirza away."

"Why do you care so much?" Jerome demanded. "The only reason you even started talking to her is because—"

Someone rapped on the door. The very colorful, very flimsy door, which clearly would not hold up for one second against a determined guard.

"The slippers," Dame Yaffa said. "Now is the time to use them."

I met her eyes, and I saw why the boys in the village had backed away. There was a cold, dark power in them that made my insides shiver. I would have backed away, too, if I'd had anywhere to go.

Fae blood, the minstrel had said.

"We don't have to draw on the slippers' full power," Dame Yaffa said. "Not yet. But you can use them to escape. I'll show you how."

"I ... I don't ..."

"You *must!*" she said urgently. "We can't let the slippers fall back into the queen's hands. I will risk anything to prevent that."

Well. If that was why she was doing this, maybe it wasn't the best time to explain that I hadn't taken them.

"I don't...have them," I managed. "I mean, not with me."

"What does that have to do with anything? *Call* them!"

I closed my eyes and tried to look like I was trying. To my astonishment, I felt something faint and distant. It brushed against my skin, a solid whisper, simmering with the promise of power and wonder.

My eyes snapped open in shock, and the tingle vanished.

This time, the knock on the door was more of a pounding. Dame Yaffa hissed through her teeth. "We're running out of time. Aden, take her out back."

Jerome snorted. "I think they might be watching the back too."

Aden dashed across the kitchen and into the common room. "No! No one out here."

"Good," Dame Yaffa said. "I'll delay the guards." Her brow furrowed. "Why are they not coming in yet?"

"Tirza!" Aden said. "Let's go."

I stood up, then quickly sat down again. My legs felt like rubber.

Jerome stepped back from the window with a sudden

curse. "Oh. That's who they were waiting for. Tirza, you need to go *now*."

Another knock at the door. Lighter than the guards', but still firm.

I tried to think. Dame Yaffa was only helping me because she believed I had the slippers, which I didn't. Once she found that out, she might not be on my side anymore. Meanwhile, if I went with Aden and got caught, I would *never* get the queen to believe I was innocent.

Then again, I hadn't done a great job of convincing her until now.

"Go!" Dame Yaffa shouted, and my body decided for me. I bolted into the common room.

"Quick!" Aden said. He was standing on a chair next to a very small, very high window. He pulled himself up and through it in a quick, lithe motion.

I heard a crash from the other side, a muffled "Ouch!" and then "It's fine! I just didn't realize this bush had thorns."

I hopped onto the chair and grabbed the windowsill. I would have to pull myself up through the window without seeing what was on the other side.

"I'll catch you!" Aden whispered. "If I can!"

That didn't make me feel better.

A creak from the kitchen as the front door opened. My arm muscles tensed.

"Dame Yaffa," Queen Ella said in a voice like ice. "Please step aside."

I glanced over my shoulder. I couldn't see the queen, which meant she couldn't see me. Yet.

It wasn't too late. I could walk through that door, walk up to the queen, and tell her the truth. Nobody else would have to be punished on my account. And as for me . . .

As for me, deep down, I still didn't believe Queen Ella would hurt me.

That's stupid. And just *how* stupid became clear in the next second, when Queen Ella said, "You know, the punishment for helping a traitor escape is death."

"Your Majesty," Dame Yaffa said. "Welcome to my humble abode."

"Tirza!" Queen Ella shouted, and I found myself leaning in her direction, about to hop off the chair.

"You're too late." Dame Yaffa laughed a small, vicious laugh. "I warned you about this. Those slippers were never meant to be worn once a year at a dance. The power in them could help the whole kingdom if only they were worn by the right person. And you, *Cinderella*, were never the right person."

I froze. No one was allowed to call the queen *Cinderella*, and certainly not to her face. It was such a strictly kept rule that I didn't even know the punishment for breaking it. I had never heard anyone break it.

Another rustle of silk, and before I could move, the queen stood in the doorway to the common room. Her face was white, and her chin was trembling, but her eyes were cold and clear.

"Get down, Tirza," she said. "You're coming with me."

11

I gripped the windowsill with all my might and pulled myself up. Queen Ella rushed across the room. Her nails dug into my calf, and I yanked harder. Then I slid out through the small window, scraping half my skin off in the process, and landed face-first in the thorn bush below.

Aden didn't apologize for not catching me. He just grabbed my hand and pulled me across a scraggly patch of grass and into the woods behind the cottage. We crashed blindly through the underbrush. Branches whipped my face, leaving behind a hundred stinging scratches.

"Stop!" a guard shouted, and I tried to speed up. My foot caught on an exposed root. I lurched forward and grabbed Aden's arm, which slowed me down enough to land on my knees instead of on my face. One of my calves hit a rock and pain shot up my leg. I screamed.

"Quiet!" Aden gasped, but it was too late. I heard the guards right behind us, snapping twigs and breaking branches. One of them swore—apparently, he'd gotten into the thorns too.

"Tirza!" Aden said frantically. "Get up!"

"Go!" I said. I clearly wasn't going to make it in time. "Aden, *go!*"

"We'll come back for you," Aden promised, then turned and raced off through the trees.

I had kind of expected him to argue. I would have nobly ordered him to leave anyhow—there was no reason for him to get caught too—but still, a *bit* of hesitation before he abandoned me would have been nice.

The guard grabbed me by the shoulders and yanked me upright. He dragged me through the bushes—apparently without thinking about the fact that they were just as thorny on the way back—then whirled me around to face the queen.

Who was standing on the grass, safely away from the thorns, her arms crossed over her chest. Two other guards stood on either side of her. Neither Dame Yaffa nor Jerome was anywhere to be seen.

"I wish it hadn't come to this," the queen said. "Guards, tie her hands behind her back and put her into the coach."

The guard who had grabbed me was happy to obey.

He probably would have preferred to use chains, if he'd had any handy, but the pieces of twine he produced were itchy and uncomfortable, and he tied them far tighter than was necessary. He didn't have any scratches on his face, which made sense—he was a lot taller than me—but which I found disappointing.

His *hands* were scratched up, though. I tried to take comfort in that.

"What are you smirking about?" the guard demanded. "You won't be so happy when we get through with you, I can tell you that."

"I know you can," I said. "Because you just did. But that doesn't actually make it true."

The guard spat in my face, and his spittle landed on my cheek. I could feel it dripping toward my mouth, and with my hands tied behind my back, I had no way to stop it.

"There was no need for that," Queen Ella said sharply.

"Sorry," the guard said, not sounding very sorry.

The queen came over and used the edge of her silk sleeve to wipe the guard's saliva from my face. I did my best not to meet her eyes, but once she was done, she didn't move away. My neck started to hurt from the weird angle I was forcing it into, but it still seemed better than looking her in the face.

"I don't know what Dame Yaffa told you," the queen

said finally. "But you can't trust her. I learned that the hard way."

My neck was *really* hurting, and my gaze was unfortunately focused on a patch of bird poop on the cottage's roof, but I maintained my position. I was hot with shame, and not only because the queen had just wiped spittle off my face.

"She calls herself a faerie," the queen said, "and the villagers believe it. They're not entirely wrong—everyone around here has some fae blood in them, from the time long ago when faeries and humans mingled freely in this part of the world. It was strongest in the royal family, but every once in a while, the faerie traits show up strongly in someone from the village. Sometimes it's a particular gift for art or music or dance. Sometimes it shows in the smallness of their feet. And sometimes they have an affinity for magic." She paused. "That, of course, is the one that really matters."

I had learned some of this in my history lessons. I knew that Tarel was the only one of the Twelve Kingdoms that still had magic. I knew it was our magic that kept us safe from our larger, more powerful neighbors. But I had never realized that this was also why our kingdom was famous for its artwork and music or put it together with the reason everyone thought small feet were pretty.

"I have a gift for magic," the queen said. "But I never realized it until Dame Yaffa gave my stepmother those slippers, and I felt them singing under my skin."

I forgot myself and turned to face her. *Singing under my skin*—that was exactly what it had felt like.

The queen met my eyes and smiled, with that expression of fierce pride I hated, as if my looking at her was a victory. And my neck didn't even feel any better.

"I didn't realize how strong the fae blood was in you either," she said. "Until now. It's why I don't blame you for stealing the slippers." She blinked, her brown eyes large and compelling. I felt like a bird held in thrall by a snake. "I know how they call to you. They call to me the same way. But they're dangerous, Tirza. You can't trust the way they make you feel."

I looked away again, despite my neck's protests, so the queen wouldn't see *my* expression. She was wrong. I felt the same way I had *always* felt: fierce and trapped and angry. The only difference was that now I was letting it show.

"I'm not angry at you," the queen said. "Truly, I'm not. I'm sorry I lost my temper earlier."

I laughed. The sound surprised me—both the laugh itself and the way it came out. Short and hard and jagged. I met the queen's soft, tear-filled eyes. She had switched to her earnest, innocent expression, so unnaturally sweet that even I had almost been taken in by it. *That* was the feeling I couldn't trust: the queen's charm. She had used the slippers' power to enchant a prince and a nation into loving her. And she had made me love her too.

"If you're not angry," I said, "why are my hands tied up?"

"Because," the guard growled, "you've proved you can't be trusted."

The queen silenced him with a look and then turned to me. "I'm giving you one last chance, Tirza. The ball is tomorrow night. If I don't wear the glass slippers, then ..." Once again, I saw fear on her face. "It won't be only me who suffers."

And that, clearly, was a threat.

"I can't give them back," I said. "I didn't take them, and I don't know where they are."

Fury flared in Queen Ella's eyes, so fierce it burned the tears away.

"Stop it, Tirza," she said. "Just *stop*. Dame Yaffa already told me that you have them."

I had no response for that.

She stepped away from me. Every trace of her pretend softness was gone. Her face could have been carved from ice.

"Take her to the castle," she said. "This time, make sure she doesn't escape before the king and I are ready to deal with her."

12

The castle dungeon had not been used for as long as I could remember. In fact, Aden and I used to play hide-and-seek in the dark passageways and deserted cells, until the time we accidentally triggered a hidden trap and got caught behind a wall lined with spikes. The spikes weren't a problem—they had been meant to impale much bigger people than us, and we avoided them easily—but some devious torturer had also, at some point, started breeding extra-large spiders to go along with them.

After we were found, we were given a *very* strict talking-to, which was entirely unnecessary. Even Aden never suggested we play there again.

"I'm pretty sure," I said desperately, as the guard pulled open the heavy door that led beneath the castle, "that the queen didn't mean you should put me down *there*."

"Where else do you think traitors go?" the guard

sneered. He put one hand on my back and shoved so hard I almost fell down the steep stairway. "Get moving."

I had to grab the wall twice more before we got to my cell, even though the guard didn't push me again. They were narrow, slippery steps. Anyone would have lost their footing at least once. Which meant *I* was guaranteed to lose it twice.

Luckily, my cell was the first one at the bottom of the stairs. Which made sense—the dungeon was, after all, empty—but I wouldn't have put it past the guard to put me as deep in the dungeon as he could. Maybe he didn't like the sight of that damp, narrow corridor any more than I did. He had probably heard the minstrel's song about the spiders, "On Many Legs."

(The song had really been about me. Luckily for the minstrel, *spider* rhymed with *outsider*.)

The guard untied my wrists, pushed me in, and slammed my cell door shut. The boom echoed through the darkness. It was so loud I couldn't make out whatever else he said before he turned and left.

Which was probably for the best.

I waited until he was gone. (He also shut the door at the top of the stairs with a clang; maybe he was just bad at closing doors). Then I examined my prison cell by the faint light coming in through the single narrow window near the ceiling.

 100

Small. Dark. Awful-smelling. No surprises there; Aden and I had dashed in and out of plenty of cells just like this. I didn't see any spiders, which was a good sign. We had never seen any this close to the surface, and that trap we'd triggered had been two levels down. Even so, I carefully inspected the narrow straw cot near the wall before I sat on it.

Just your standard dungeon cell where people were sent to languish and die.

Except no one *had* been sent here for years. The queen didn't allow it. And she wouldn't leave me here, either, not for long. Once she got over her anger, she would let me out.

Even if I won't tell her where the slippers are?

The straw was dry and dusty—probably a consequence of the dungeon being left unused—and I sneezed several times. My sneezes were very loud, but they didn't scare any spiders into the open. Another good sign.

I wrapped my arms around my knees and waited for Queen Ella to come get me out.

———◆———

By the time the door at the top of the stairs opened, I had realized another consequence of the dungeon's disuse: There was no chamber pot in my cell. I stood up, more eager than afraid, as light illuminated the doorway at the top of the stairs.

I was distracted by my need for a chamber pot, or I would have realized right away that the silhouette coming down the stairs wasn't the queen. She was too short, and her footsteps were heavier and less graceful. She even lost her balance at one point and had to put her hand against the wall to catch herself.

But it wasn't until she came right up to the bars of my cell that I realized who she was.

"Gilma," I said. "How nice of you to visit."

Gilma's lips curved into a smirk. "I wouldn't have missed it for the world."

I couldn't come up with a retort. I was too busy trying to figure out why she was here.

"I guess the queen has finally seen you for what you really are," Gilma went on. "All those years of her letting you get away with everything, choosing you over those who were *truly* loyal to her . . . And you couldn't be content with what you had, could you? You had to push it until even she could no longer be blind to how wicked you are."

"That's a really good speech," I said. "Did you practice it all the way here?"

"I've been practicing it for *years*. I knew this day would come." She leaned closer to the bars. "How could I resist watching you finally get what you deserve?"

"Apparently," I said, "you couldn't. But now that you've seen me, feel free to leave."

"Oh, I'm not here alone. The queen isn't the only one who needs to see the truth about you." She turned to the stairs, which were black and shiny in the light from the doorway, and made a beckoning motion. "Come down, Baro."

My stomach turned inside out. "Are you crazy? You're bringing the crown prince into the dungeon?"

"He sneaked out of bed and followed me." Gilma wasn't a very good liar; she always sounded like she was practicing her story. *I didn't realize it was dye! I thought it was shampoo!*

I wanted to reach through the bars and strangle her. But she was, wisely, staying out of reach.

"Don't be scared," she called up the stairs. "I won't let her hurt you."

A small figure appeared in the doorway at the top of the stairs.

I stepped away from the bars until my back hit the wall. If Baro looked at me the way everyone else in the castle did, as if I was wicked and contemptible ...

I hated Gilma more than I had ever hated anyone in my life.

Baro started down the stairs, and I pressed against the stones, as if I could melt into them and disappear.

"You'll be sorry for this," I hissed, and Gilma laughed.

"What are they going to do? Humiliate me publicly? I survived it the first time. I think I can manage again."

"I didn't ask the queen to do that! And also, it was *four years ago*! You need to get over it."

"I'm trying to," Gilma said. "I think this will really help."

I clenched my fists, unable to think of a comeback. Or of a way to stop Baro from coming down those stairs and seeing me behind bars.

"Tirza?" he said in a wobbly uncertain voice, and a tingle sizzled along my skin. It was so strong that I straightened in shock, and so unmistakable that I didn't think, even for a second, that I had imagined it.

But how could the slippers be *here*?

"Baro?" I said, and the sudden change in my tone made Gilma turn her head. "Are you—are you bringing me something?"

"You're not to bring her anything," Gilma snapped. "She's a criminal."

"No, she's not!" Baro said.

My heart pounded against my ribs, my skin prickling all over. The dungeon seemed full of a wild, charged stillness, like the coming of a storm. "That's right, Baro," I said as calmly as I could. "I'm not a criminal. Some people have made a mistake."

"It's no mistake." Gilma glared up the stairs. "Your own father, the king, said she's a traitor! He declared it to the whole court. Do you think your father *lied*, Baro?"

"My mother yelled at him," Baro protested. His voice wobbled again. "She told him not to say that."

"But he did," Gilma said, "because it's true. Tirza has been fooling you all along. She's been fooling everyone, but we know better now, don't we? She stole your mother's slippers!"

"*I* didn't get punished when *I* tried to take them! It's not fair!"

Something warm swelled in my chest, displacing the spark of the slippers' nearness. "Don't worry, Baro," I said, at the same time that Gilma said, "You're the crown prince! It's not the same—"

"What is going on?" The door at the top of the stairs was flung wide-open, and the light—which had seemed dim when I was brought here—was suddenly blinding. I didn't recognize the voice of the noblewoman at the door, but it was even shriller than Gilma's. "Baro! What are you thinking?"

I squinted. In the light, I could clearly see Baro's blue pajamas, his round, red-cheeked face, and his empty hands. He was wearing indoor slippers made of cloth.

And the tingling was gone. The only thing I felt running along my skin was the heat of humiliation.

 105

The slippers were gone. Or more likely, they had never been here. How *could* they have been? It had just been my imagination mingled with my desperation.

"Come with me at once!" The noblewoman rushed down the stairs, grabbed Baro's arm, and hauled him up into the rectangle of light. "You don't belong down here."

"I *do*!" Baro howled, and then the noblewoman slammed the door shut.

"Well," I said. Even though I had barely moved, I was drenched in sweat. "I guess that didn't work out the way you planned."

Gilma's shoulders twitched, but her voice was cool. "Things still worked out better for me than they did for you."

While I was futilely trying to think of a response to that, she dashed up the stairs. She opened the door just far enough to let in a thin line of light before slamming it shut and plunging me back into darkness.

13

I don't know how long I waited in the dungeon after that. Long enough to think of five devastating comebacks I could have made to Gilma. And then long enough that my need for the chamber pot became the only thing I could think about.

By the time the door creaked open again, I would have been one hundred percent willing to tell the queen where the slippers were in exchange for a chance to use the privy. Except that I still didn't know where the slippers were.

And except that, once again, the person coming down the stairs wasn't the queen.

"Aden!" I whispered. "What are you doing here?"

"What do you think?" Aden came to a stop in front of my cell and held up a large, rusty key. "I'm getting you out."

"Where did you get that? And how did you get past the guard?"

Aden smirked. "Do you know how little the castle guards get paid? The queen is too convinced that her people love her. Because of that, she doesn't pay them enough to buy their loyalty."

"You bribed the guard?" Then it hit me. "You bribed the guard outside my room, too, when you came with the message from my sisters. He was never asleep."

"Of course."

"But how?" I asked. "Where did *you* get enough money to buy anyone's loyalty?"

"From Dame Yaffa, of course." He chewed at the corner of his lips as he knelt and examined the lock. "She's been in touch with your sisters ever since they were banished, and now that you have the slippers, she believes the time has come to act. Together you can wrong the rights, I mean, undo the wrongs—I don't remember her exact words. But it was very inspiring."

I felt entirely uninspired. "I don't have the slippers, Aden. You know that."

"*I* know that," Aden said. "But Dame Yaffa doesn't. She thinks you stole the queen's slippers, and that's why she's willing to help you. So why don't we let her keep believing it?"

"Because eventually she'll find out that I don't have them!"

"By then," Aden said, "you'll be out of the dungeon."

He had a point.

"Can we discuss this later?" Aden asked. "That guard isn't going to stay bribed forever."

I hesitated, still sure that he wasn't telling me everything. Then again, I *really* needed a chamber pot.

Aden wasn't waiting for my answer, anyhow. He inserted the rusty key into the lock and turned it. Or tried to turn it. It immediately stuck.

Honestly. Just because they hadn't used the dungeon in years, did that mean they had to let the place go entirely?

"Argh," Aden said, trying to force the key. "Don't worry. I'll get it open."

"Why would I worry?" I asked.

"Exactly!" He wrenched the key so hard that his hand slid off it and hit one of the bars of my cell. "Ouch! I mean, I'm fine. That was part of my method."

"Your hand is bleeding," I pointed out.

"It's just a scratch." He winced. "A painful scratch."

"A *dangerous* scratch!" I said. "That key is rusty."

"Don't worry. Dame Yaffa can cure it." He set his jaw. "I won't give up until I get you out."

"Why?" I asked.

He went back to trying to get the key to turn. "What do you mean, *why?*"

"Why are you helping me? You could end up imprisoned for treason. Why would you take such a chance?"

"That's a ridiculous question." Aden jerked at the key. "I'm your friend!"

"Why are you my friend?"

Aden sighed. He seemed nervous, but maybe that was because he couldn't get the key to so much as jiggle. "This feels a lot like having a conversation with Baro."

"Don't avoid the question. Why did *you* decide to like me? Everyone else in this castle believes I'm wicked. Don't tell me you didn't start out thinking the same thing."

Aden looked up at last, still wiggling ineffectually at the key. "I did start out that way. But now I know that you're not wicked. You're *good*. Even if no one else sees it, I see it."

"But what made you *look* for it?" I demanded. "Everyone you know thinks I'm awful. What made you decide they might be wrong?"

The key turned with a sudden wrench. Aden let out a breath of relief. "Finally. Let's get to Dame Yaffa, and she can explain."

"Explain what?" I demanded. "Why she ordered you to be my friend?"

The door to my cell swung open. The seconds ticked by, slow and silent.

Until then, I had held on to a faint hope that my

suspicion wasn't true. But the expression on Aden's face shattered that hope into a thousand shards.

"So that's why," I said. The shards were cutting me up, and their sharpness came out in my voice. "You only acted like my friend because Dame Yaffa told you to. Did she . . . did she *pay* you?" I realized the answer a second after I asked. "She paid you in baked goods. In return for your spying on me, she bakes you cupcakes to sell in the castle."

Aden looked down. "Back when Dame Yaffa approached me, I didn't even know you. Why wouldn't I agree? But now I would be your friend no matter what."

"Why did she approach you, Aden? What did she want you to do, once you got me to trust you?"

"Nothing!" Aden said. "She just wanted me to keep watch over you and make sure you were safe. So she could tell your sisters how you were doing."

"My sisters?"

"Yes. Did you really think they would abandon you to the queen? They don't dare leave Larosia, but Dame Yaffa keeps them updated about you. They're your family, Tirza. They were trying to make sure you were safe."

I laughed, short and bitter. "You must have worked really hard to convince yourself of that."

"Don't believe all the stories about your sisters. The

queen exaggerated everything. She took normal sibling rivalry and painted it as evil so she could get away with what she did to them. Dame Yaffa will tell you; she'll explain. Once we get to the village—"

"We're not going to the village," I said.

"What?" Aden almost dropped the key. "Tirza, I know you're upset, but you can't stay here. King Ciaran has publicly announced that he will try you for treason. He can't take that back, no matter how much the queen begs him to."

"I'm not staying here either," I said.

He rubbed the back of his neck. "There's nowhere else for you to go."

"Isn't there?" I felt a wash of something like relief. Aden was right about one thing: Everything I knew about my sisters, everything *any*one knew, I had heard from the queen. She had done it on purpose, to make me feel all alone, like she was the only one I could depend on. But it had never been true. My sisters had been watching me all along. And even if I didn't exactly approve of their methods . . .

They're your family.

You are not alone.

"Take me to the harbor," I said. "I'm going to Larosia to rejoin my family."

14

There were no chamber pots in the dungeon, but there *were* some grates farther down the corridor that probably fed right into the sewers. Don't judge me, okay? (At least, not for that.) I was *very* desperate.

Aden judged me—I could tell by his expression when I rejoined him at the bottom of the stairs. But he wisely decided not to say anything.

There was no guard at the top of the staircase, and it was so late by now that the wall torches weren't lit. Though the moon was bright, barely any of its light filtered through the windows. I had to concentrate hard to follow Aden without walking into a wall or tripping and falling. Which was good, because it didn't leave me enough time to feel those shards of betrayal still cutting me into painful pieces, or to think about where we were going and whether I should be doing this and—

"Who goes there?" a voice shouted in the darkness.

Aden stopped so suddenly that I ran into him. He pitched onto his hands and knees, letting out a squawk that could have woken the entire castle.

"Stop!" The voice was fierce and gravelly, and had the aggressive, confident edge of a man holding a sword. "Show yourself."

"It's just me," Aden called, getting to his feet. "Aden, the stable boy. I'm alone."

I had been about to step up next to him. I froze.

"Aden?" A circle of torchlight appeared around the bend, illuminating the guard holding it. I crept backward, but the guard stopped moving as soon as the circle of light encompassed Aden.

I resisted the urge to continue moving back. As long as I didn't make any sound to alert the guard to my presence, he wouldn't know I was there.

"What are you doing here?" the guard demanded. "Are you coming from the *dungeon*?"

"Queen Ella wanted me to bring Tirza some cookies," Aden said.

Disgust flickered across the guard's face. "There are some orders you shouldn't obey. We've all seen how that girl repays those who do her kindness. There's nothing to be gained from having anything to do with her."

"I know that," Aden said. "And I *didn't* obey."

The guard paused. "So ... you still have the cookies?"

"What do you think?"

"If you got them from Dame Yaffa, I think you ate them."

Aden smirked. "I couldn't resist. But I bet the queen will want me to bring more tomorrow."

"I'll be stationed in the courtyard tomorrow night."

"I'll remember that," Aden said solemnly. "And I'll give you a discount."

The guard laughed and then shook his head. "But honestly, Queen Ella should know better. Some people are rotten at their core. Hold out your hand in sympathy, and they'll bite it off."

"I'll tell Her Majesty that," Aden said. "But *after* tomorrow's cookies."

The guard grinned and turned. The circle of light passed from Aden's face and grew fainter. I heard the *clump-clump* of boots as the guard went on down the hallway.

Aden, however, moved so quietly that I didn't realize he was next to me until he spoke. "Ready to go?"

There was no hint of sympathy in his voice. It was like he hadn't even heard the things the guard said about me.

Except of course he had. It was just that he had heard them a million times before, so he saw no reason to make special mention of this time.

"Tirza?" Aden whispered. "We need to move. I don't know who else we might run into."

"Right," I said. Amazingly, my voice had only the faintest quiver, and as far as Aden knew, that could have been from the close call with the guard. "I'm ready. Let's go."

The way to the castle harbor was through a long, unlit passageway that ended in a bolted door. The bolt creaked alarmingly as we slid it out, and it took both of us pushing with all our might to get the door open. The castle harbor hadn't been used in years—six years, to be exact. The only thing across this stretch of water was the barren mountain range of the Larosian peninsula. Shortly after exiling my sisters, Queen Ella had decreed that criminals would no longer be banished across the ocean. She preferred to let people "rehabilitate" themselves and "rejoin society."

Once we got the door slightly open, Aden and I slipped through onto the top of a cliff. Below us, the sea looked like a dark flat plain, the illusion broken only by the sudden, startling leaps of white spray. The moonlight gleamed on the distant black ridges of the Larosian cliffs.

A narrow stairway was cut into the cliffside, as steep and slick as I remembered. I started down.

I forced myself not to check if Aden was following. Luckily, the night was so still that I could hear his feet thudding against the stone—at least until we got close to the water, and the roar of the waves drowned out both our footsteps.

A single boat was tied up against the shore, covered with a thick, heavy black tarp. The sight of it made me feel like I was going to throw up.

Aden stepped off the stairs. "Have you thought this through? That boat is too big for you to row by yourself."

"Of course I haven't thought it through," I snapped. "I came up with this plan ten minutes ago."

"Oh, are we calling it a plan, now?"

The boat *was* big, but not as large as in my memory. The tarp rustled in the wind like some sort of vast black creature.

I shivered. My family had been taken away on this boat. I could *see* the shore where they had landed from my window. Yet I had never come near this harbor after that day, when Cinderella had led me away and promised I would be safe. I had been too busy putting on silk dresses and worrying about courtiers making petty comments about me. Meanwhile, my sisters—my *real* sisters—had been suffering in exile, and I hadn't even tried to rescue them.

Well, what were they expecting? I argued with myself. *I was only five years old! And I'm only eleven now.*

But the guilt couldn't be argued with. It sat like a rock

in my gut, impervious to reason. As it had all these years, while I had done my best to pretend it wasn't there.

"Help me get the tarp off," I said.

"But—"

I was angry at myself, which somehow made me even angrier at Aden. "Maybe Dame Yaffa will pay you extra for it. Or double the frosting for your next batch of cupcakes."

Aden sighed, bent, and began untying the knots that held the tarp down. "For the record, I think this is a stupid idea."

"Then why are you helping me?"

"To prove that I'm your friend!"

"Would a true friend help their friend do something stupid?"

He untied the next knot. "What exactly are you trying to argue? I think—AUGH!"

The tarp whipped up, hitting him in the face. He stumbled and sat down as a gust of wind lifted the tarp up.

"Sorry!" he said, scrambling to his feet. "I didn't expect—"

Canvas scraped loudly against wood, and the tarp flew off the boat and landed on top of us.

I screamed. The tarp flailed around me, thick and

heavy. I tried to turn, and it wrapped around my legs like a living thing. I pitched backward and thudded to the ground with an impact that knocked the breath out of me.

The tarp billowed as the wind blew it back. Instead of being blown away, though, it flapped around me, pressing me to the ground. I kicked at it futilely.

"Tirza!" Aden shouted. "You need to roll out from under it!"

I obeyed blindly, tucking my arms against my chest and rolling. Then the wind died, and the tarp came suddenly down on me. Heavy, suffocating canvas pressed against my face, blocking the breath I needed to scream.

The wind whistled by, the tarp lifted again, and I rolled as fast as I could. One of the hooks under the tarp caught my calf, and I ripped my leg free with a stab of agony.

Two hands clasped my wrists, and Aden pulled me out, scraping my whole body against rocks. He yanked me to my feet, away from the tarp.

"Are you all right?" he gasped.

"I—" A line of pain sizzled up my leg. A thin, shallow cut zigzagged along my calf, trickling blood. "I ... We need to get out of here, before—"

The wind hit me in the face, throwing gritty sand

between my teeth. The tarp thrashed behind us, and I whirled so fast I bumped into Aden. The tarp blew away and slammed, wetly and heavily, into the sea.

A group of seagulls flapped up away from the splash, squawking in outrage. They sounded a lot like *I* had when that thing was coming at me.

Aden and I stared at each other, wild-eyed and breathless. Then he started to laugh.

"It's not *funny!*" I shouted. But I was also laughing. The seagulls fled over our heads in a black-tinged white mass, scolding furiously, and we both doubled over, holding our sides. I was laughing so hard my cheeks hurt.

Aden's laugh turned into a choked gurgling sound, and then, by some process that made no sense, into a sneeze. He clutched his stomach, staring over my shoulder, and his expression changed. "Tirza."

"I can't!" I managed to get out. My head ached from laughing. "It's just too—"

"Tirza!"

The panic in his voice stopped my laughter cold. I whirled to see what he was looking at.

A tall, slim figure raced down the stairway to the harbor, her golden hair streaming behind her in the wind.

15

Aden's face was white. His lips barely moved as he spoke. "I guess we should have tried to be quieter."

"It will be all right," I said, then realized that it wouldn't be. Not for him. *He* was not connected to the royal family; he didn't have any knowledge they needed; he had no claim on the queen's affection—or on her pretend affection.

And the dungeon was back in use.

"Go," I said. "She's too far away to see you clearly." At least, I hoped she was. "Go around the edge of the castle and get to the village. *Now!*"

He turned and ran.

It occurred to me that I could follow him. But there was only one place in the village I could go, and the queen would easily find me there and have me arrested again.

Where would she escape to? the minstrel had asked, and the answer was still the same. Nowhere.

So I stood there, the black boat to my right, the ocean roaring at my back, and watched the queen sweep down the stairs toward me.

"Tirza," she said, coming to a stop on the bottom stair. "What are you doing?"

Rage coiled in my stomach. Now that I knew how angry I was, I couldn't seem to control it. I was furious at the queen for falsely accusing me, but also for everything else. For the sneers she could have stopped but didn't. For the way she always pretended to be kind, but it was only for the sake of appearances. And most of all, for the fact that she had, at times, fooled me into thinking she loved me.

"Isn't it obvious?" I said. "I'm escaping." (Although clearly "*trying* to escape" would have been more accurate.) "No offense. It's just that the dungeon was missing a few amenities."

The queen's face turned pink. "I'm sorry, Tirza. I didn't know you were in the dungeon until Baro told me. I went to release you, but you were already gone."

"How kind of you," I said. "I'm glad I was able to save you the trouble."

Queen Ella flinched.

"You think I'm lying?" she said.

I knew better than to say what I thought. . . . At least, a part of me did. But I was still too angry to be afraid. In my mind, I kept hearing Dame Yaffa say *Cinderella* in a tone of utter contempt. She, too, saw the queen for what she really was.

"Yes," I said. "But that's no different from usual. I think you're always lying. And I'm the only one who can tell."

A brief stricken expression crossed Queen Ella's face before she drew herself up.

"And why do you think that is?" she demanded. "Do you think it's because you're so much smarter than everyone else? That no one but you is perceptive enough to see how terrible I am?"

"Yes," I said.

"I assure you you're not. That nasty look you're giving me right now? You used to look at me like that when you were five years old too. Just copying your mother."

And that, clearly, was a threat. *What I did to your mother, I can do to you.*

"I gave up a lot to escape from that house," the queen said, "and to take you with me. I gave up the only home I had ever known. I gave up my freedom when I tied myself to those slippers. You must know by now how much power they have over you once you've put them on." I stared at her stonily, and she sighed. "But I never thought I was giving up *you.*"

She sounded like she was about to cry. *It's a trick,* I

reminded myself, *just like her smiles.* It was a better, *smarter* trick—I felt my defenses melting—but it was just another ploy the queen had practiced for a long time.

The worst thing was that a part of me warmed in response. That I wanted to be fooled by her, and had always wanted to be.

"It's my fault, I suppose," Queen Ella went on. "I meant to spend so much more time with you. But you were so angry with me, Tirza. It made it difficult to be around you. And learning to be queen took up all of my attention, for so long. I shouldn't have let it. But maybe it's not too late."

Something twisted deep in my gut. "As long as I give back the slippers?" I asked.

The queen sat on one of the lower stairs, spreading her skirts around her.

"I understand the pull the slippers have on you," she said. "I've been fighting them ever since that first ball. Even after a mere evening of dancing in them, it took all my strength to leave one of them behind for the prince to find. I should have left them both, but . . ." She bit her lip. "I couldn't bear to give both of them up. You understand that, I think."

She raised her eyebrows, like we shared a secret. I fought not to let my expression change.

"I went to the ball because of you, you know," she said. "Because I found out their plans for the slippers. They intended for you to wear them, once you were older."

That memory again: The slipper sliding onto my little foot. The happiness in my mother's voice.

"By then, they would have trained you, taught you to be exactly like them. You would have been a willing pawn in their schemes." The queen hunched her shoulders. "I ruined that for them."

"How kind of you," I said.

Something fierce flashed in her eyes. "I'm not saying I didn't want to. I could feel the slippers, singing under my skin. And they were so easy to steal. Nobody in that house ever thought I would do something like that. They never thought about me at all." For a moment, her eyes were wide and lost, and I could see the helpless, unloved child she must once have been. "They couldn't believe it when they realized what I had done. They held me down and took the remaining slipper from me, and that was when your mother got desperate enough to try on the slipper herself, and . . ." She stopped and lowered her head. Then she straightened, her eyes hard, and she looked again like the queen.

"But they should have thought about me," she said. "That was their mistake." She tilted her head and examined me. "And I made the same mistake, didn't I? I should have thought more about you."

Behind me the waves pounded into the sand, over and over.

"Things will change, Tirza, I promise. Even if you don't give back the slippers."

"I can't give them back," I said. "I don't have them. You have to believe me." All at once, my chin felt dangerously wobbly. I pressed my lips together so the queen wouldn't be able to tell.

"All right," Queen Ella said. She rose and held out her hand. "I believe you."

Her eyes brimmed with tears. I had a sudden, violent memory of staring into her face as those tears spilled down her cheeks. Of throwing my small spindly arms around her ash-stained neck.

It will be all right, Ella. I'll stay with you!

The queen blinked, and a single tear rolled down her cheek. "Maybe it's for the best that the slippers are gone."

"What about the kingdom?" I demanded. "Don't we need the magic from the slippers to protect ourselves?"

"Maybe," Queen Ella said. "Or maybe if we weren't depending so much on magic, we would think of another way to handle our problems."

If we had another way, you wouldn't be queen, I thought.

I took her hand. Her slim, elegant fingers closed

around mine. "We need to get you to bed, Tirza. Tomorrow night, you're going to a ball."

My vision was blurry, as if I was going to cry too. "But I'm never allowed to go to the ball."

"Maybe that was a mistake," the queen said. "I was trying to protect you from the slippers. You tried them on once, and I knew they must still have a hold on you." She managed a shaky smile. "But I've been thinking about it for a while, and I believe you're ready. I had a dress made for you weeks ago, one that matches mine. I was going to talk to Ciaran about it . . ."

I snorted.

She shook her head. "He's a good king, Tirza. He's been trained since birth to be ruthless in the defense of his kingdom, but that's what a kingdom *needs*. And he's a good husband, even though I didn't end up having the power he had hoped for. He's never held that against me. He protects his own. Someday, he'll realize that you're part of our family too. When we walk into the ball together, everyone will see—"

"STOP!" the king roared, and we both whirled.

King Ciaran stood at the top of the staircase with one arm raised. The wind whipped his cape sideways, wrapping it around his body and revealing the graceful, deadly curve of what he was holding. A bow with an arrow nocked into it.

The king was an *excellent* shot. He had won every archery contest he ever entered, even when he played against visiting royalty who didn't go easy on him.

He had always wanted to get rid of me. And here was his chance.

"Step away from her, Ella," he called. His voice shook with rage.

The sea crashed against the shore. Panic surged through me, and with it came an unexpected, familiar tingle that raced through my bones and burst into my blood.

Startled, I glanced down at the queen's feet. But she wasn't wearing the glass slippers. She was wearing thin bedroom slippers.

Yet the wild energy whipping through me was unmistakable. It felt so close too. If it wasn't coming from the queen, then where . . .

I wrenched my hand out of the queen's, took three quick steps backward, and leaned over the side of the boat.

"Stay where you are!" the king shouted.

I stared in disbelief.

Laid out neatly on the front seat of the boat, sparkling brilliantly against the black wood, were the queen's glass slippers.

16

I gaped down at the slippers, my breath tangled in my throat. Exhilaration whirled through me, so mingled with terror that I couldn't tell the difference between them. I wished the tarp was still there so I could pull it over the slippers and hide them.

But the tarp was sinking slowly into the ocean. And I couldn't move.

"Tirza!" the queen said, grabbing my arm. "I won't let him—" Her voice stopped short, the last word twisting in shock.

The slippers lay side by side, gleaming brightly, just as they had in the queen's bedroom.

"Tirza," Queen Ella whispered. "What have you done?"

"I didn't—" My voice shook so hard I could hardly get the words out. "I didn't know they were here."

Her horrified expression didn't change. Maybe because my voice was so low that she couldn't hear me over the rush and murmur of the sea. Or maybe because she could hear me, but why would she believe me? I had been caught red-handed trying to flee the castle with the slippers I had stolen.

How could the slippers be here? Under that heavy tarp that clearly hadn't been moved in years? Glistening invitingly, as if they had been polished yesterday. Perfect and magical and *mine*.

My heart was trying to beat its way out of my ribs, to escape my body before the king's arrow pierced it. But strength surged into me from the slippers, like a cool, strong breeze through muggy air, the first hint of a coming storm.

The queen had almost made me forget everything I had learned about her and about myself. I had nearly traded it all for a smile and a memory. But now the power of the slippers filled the air, a sizzle that danced along my skin, and my mind was clear. I pulled away from her, and her flinch had no power over me.

I pulled the slippers out of the boat with trembling hands. Sparks jumped from the glass to my fingertips, and something in me leapt up to meet the magic, as if it was a long-lost part of me. I kicked off my satin shoes.

"Tirza!" The queen grabbed for me again, and I dashed away, running barefoot over sand and pebbles to the other side of the boat. If any of the sharp rocks hurt the soles of my feet, I didn't feel it. "Don't! You don't understand! They're *dangerous!*"

I believed her. The slippers *felt* dangerous; the power from them filled my hands and flowed up my arms, igniting something fierce and dormant inside me. Dangerous and powerful. No wonder she had tried so hard to keep them from me.

I slipped the first one on. It fit perfectly.

"Stop!" the king shouted. "Or I'll loose this arrow!"

The second slipper fit even better.

I rose on tiptoe. The slippers moved with my feet, secure and comfortable. I had to force myself not to laugh with sheer joy.

"No!" Queen Ella cried, but it wasn't clear who she was talking to. "Tirza, please! You have to believe me—"

I turned my back on the queen and on the castle and on the arrow aimed at my heart. The moon's reflection danced on the waves—a line of silver light stretching to the horizon. A road of light and water.

I stepped out onto it.

"TIRZA!" The king and queen were screaming together now.

I took another step, and then another, onto the silver path of the moon. It hadn't turned solid—the ripples and current moved beneath my slippered feet—but I walked over it as easily as if it were a flat highway made of light.

You can use the slippers to escape, Dame Yaffa had said.

I heard the bow being drawn; the wind carried the sound to me as clear and crisp as if the king were right behind me. Strength flowed up my legs from the slippers, and I started to run.

"Don't!" Queen Ella cried, her voice a despairing wail.

My shoulder blades clenched as I waited for the whistle of the bow's release. I zigzagged as I ran, hoping to hear a splash as the arrow landed in the water behind me. But I heard nothing.

Now, with the rush and roar of the surf in my ears, I could no longer hear them screaming at me either. I felt a strange, mad urge to look back, but I didn't. Instead, I picked up my skirt and ran, over the shimmering path of light, away from the castle where everyone hated me, and toward the mist-shrouded cliffs where my real family was waiting.

17

The glass slippers filled me with energy—that same fizzy, tingling energy I had felt before, only now it was flowing through my blood instead of scratching at my skin. I ran over the moonlit water, my legs stretching longer and higher with each stride, until I felt like I was flying. The power from the slippers sizzled through me like lightning, as if it would escape my body and rip through the air. But the sky was black and clear, the moon untouched by clouds. The dark ripples and white-tipped waves flew past much faster than it normally would have been possible to run.

Which was a good thing, because the peninsula was *very* far away.

Also, running over the ocean was harder than I would have thought. (Not that I had ever given the subject much thought.) Waves kept coming at me, swelling beneath my feet and throwing me off-balance. I managed all right until I paused and glanced back at the castle rising like a shadow against the sky. I couldn't see the king and queen.

I turned back toward the peninsula just in time to see a wave rearing over me, its green underbelly surging up inches from my face. Before I had time to react, water crashed over my head with such force that it knocked me backward. Briny spray swept over me, going up my nose and stinging my eyes, and I thrashed helplessly.

But the slippers' magic seemed to extend to my whole body, keeping me from being swept under. I was able to scramble to my feet on the receding water left behind by the wave, coughing and spluttering and soaked.

After that, I learned to keep an eye on the horizon and watch for the telltale rise of oncoming waves. The trick was to rush forward and catch them early, so they met me when they were still gathering power and were merely swells I could easily step on. If I couldn't do that, I tried to meet them late enough that they had already crashed into sprays of white foam, wet but harmless. They mostly came in diagonally, so sometimes I could rush sideways and jump over a wave at its edge. It was like a dance through an unpredictable obstacle course, and it took up every bit of my concentration.

By the time the peninsula's cliffs loomed over my head, my calves felt like someone had threaded lines of fire through my muscles. But my *feet*, clad in the sparkling slippers, felt fine.

The slippers urged me to keep running, to *move*. But I made myself slow down, putting one foot carefully in front of the other, trying to give myself time to think.

The coast of the peninsula was ahead and slightly to my right, made up of steep, jagged cliffs that rose starkly from the black water. The waves beat loudly against their stony sides before falling back into the sea with roars of white fury. I had no idea how I was going to get up those cliffs.

"TIRZA!"

At first, I thought I had imagined the call. Then it came again, a trick of the ocean winds making it sound like it was right next to me.

I recognized that voice.

I turned, hopping over a gathering wave. There, at the foot of the cliff—a flash of color. A dress . . . a face . . .

"Danica?" I asked.

It had been so long since I'd said my oldest sister's name. The syllables felt foreign and forbidden on my tongue.

"Use the slippers!" This time, her tone as well as her voice was familiar. Danica had always been the smartest in our family, and she'd always had that edge of impatience, like she couldn't believe she had to constantly explain the obvious to us. "You can fly up the side of the cliff! We saw you coming, and Esme is waiting for you up there."

Esme. My other sister, my ally when Danica was on a rampage. Though usually, we had managed to turn her rages on Cinderella.

"Fly!" Danica yelled, her voice muffled by the surf. "Use the slippers! You can fly right up!"

Exhilaration flooded through me, an instinctive *yes.* I craned my neck back, staring at the line where the dark cliffs met the slightly darker sky. So, so far above me.

I had heard Queen Ella's story many times, in many guises—there were, at last count, twelve books, seven songs, three plays, countless tapestries, and one extremely elaborate sculpture about it. In none of those versions did anyone mention Queen Ella *flying* while wearing the slippers.

But maybe she hadn't tried. Maybe she hadn't wanted to fly; she had merely wanted to dance.

"Now," I whispered to the slippers, and jumped.

The side of the cliff rushed past me; the water receded beneath me. A laugh bubbled from my lips, and I spread my arms as if they were wings.

Then I fell.

I had time for one sharp scream before the cold water closed over my head. Even then, I couldn't switch my mindset from *flying* to *swimming.* I spluttered and flailed, and the waves knocked me sideways, and the cold, dark, chaotic world turned upside down. Seawater rushed into my mouth and nose. I kicked frantically until my head broke the surface.

I treaded water, gasping. Two years ago, the queen had forced me to learn how to swim, and I was glad of it now—though if Queen Ella had known the circumstances under which those lessons would come in useful, she probably would have skipped them. I stared around at the stretch of dark, surging water on one side of me and the steep black cliff on the other.

"Tirza!" Danica screamed, but I could barely hear her through the water filling my ears. I could still feel the slippers on my feet, but they were dull weights, wet and heavy, and my arms were already getting tired. In my mind, I heard my swimming instructor's voice: *If anything is weighing you down, kick it off before you start swimming.*

I gritted my teeth and swam in the direction of the cliffs. Seawater hit my face, burning down my throat and blinding my eyes. The shoes became heavier with every stroke.

When I got closer to the cliff, I saw that they weren't quite as sheer as they had seemed from a distance. Jagged cracks ran all down the length of the cliff face, and tiny beaches jutted out from the rock. But I couldn't see my sister.

Some ways off the cliffside, a few jagged boulders stuck out of the water, slick and sharp-edged. I grabbed one and tried to pull myself up. It was too slippery, but I did manage to hold on to it, giving me a brief rest from swimming. The sea surged and crashed around me, shooting billows of spray into the air.

I heard Danica's voice again—"Tirza, this way! To me!"—but I couldn't tell which direction it was coming from.

I tried to aim my thoughts at the slippers. *Lift me up! DO SOMETHING MAGICAL!*

But I couldn't even feel them. Well, obviously I could *feel* them—water had seeped inside them, making them cold and heavy—but there was no tingling, no sense of magic. If not for the fact that I had walked here on a path of moonlight, I would have thought they were an ordinary pair of shoes.

According to at least one of the stories about Cinderella, the slippers had lost their magic at midnight. I had always assumed that was an embellishment, a way to add a moral to the story—*Don't stay out dancing too late!*—but what if it was true?

Something brushed the side of my leg—something slippery and smooth and clearly *alive*. I shrieked and let go of the boulder, striking out for the cliffside.

Another slippery creature slid past my leg, and then another. Panic exploded deep in my stomach, and I swam with all my might, but I could not swim faster than a sea creature. They were all around me now, roiling the water. Something cold and sharp touched my calf and darted away, and agony shot through my leg. Whatever it was, it had bitten me.

"HELP!" I screamed. I stopped trying to swim—it was clearly useless—and instead spent my energy shouting as loud as I could. "HELP HELP HELP ME! *DANICA!*"

"I'm here!" she cried, and I turned and saw a figure swimming through the waves, a thin pale face crisscrossed with black hair.

Relief flooded through me. Danica had always been the competent and capable one, my sister who could take care of anything....

But she was still far away and not getting much closer. A wave broke over her, and I couldn't see her. Then her head emerged from the swirling water, her hair plastered in wet black strands across her face.

"Go back!" I shouted. "Get to safety!"

Her response was to redouble her efforts, but it was clear *she* had never had swimming lessons. Another wave crashed down on her, and this time it was several seconds before she reappeared.

A surge from the slippers went through me, as if the shoes were finally reacting to my terror. But it was just pain shooting up my leg. I had no magic and no power. I was going to be pulled under the waves, and the queen would never even know how I had died.

The cliffs rose black and silent above me. The water crashed against the rocks with a low boom. Around me, the sea seethed, and a fin emerged from the ripples to my left.

Shark. I stopped breathing. Then something closed around my foot—around the slipper—and I kicked with all my might.

The creature went shooting backward, churning the water, and I flew up in a spurt of spray.

Up, up, and up, the cliff face shooting past me. Far below, the spray arced and fell back into the sea with a frustrated, furious crash. I glanced down and instantly regretted it. I was so high that the sea looked like a stretch of rippled marble. If I fell now . . .

But I didn't fall. Strength and power shot through the soles of my feet, from me to the slippers and back, a hurricane of power. The top of the cliff flew past me, revealing a flat plateau. A girl in a dark cloak lay on her stomach peering over the cliffside.

I stepped forward and down. The slippers carried me in a graceful arc over thin air and onto the ground. I landed a little too hard, stumbled, and pitched to my knees.

I shifted my weight to stand, but dizziness swept over me. Somehow, instead of getting to my feet, I found myself lying flat with my face pressed to the dirt.

"Tirza?" Esme had always sounded tentative, like she was expecting someone to contradict her. "Is it you?"

I tried to say her name, but the word didn't come out. Everything wavered around me.

Her voice went higher-pitched. "Is that *blood?*"

The answer was yes to both questions. My calf was coated with wet stickiness, and that was probably not a good thing. . . .

Her hand clamped around my heel, pulling one slipper off.

I kicked, and the effort made my head swim. Esme pulled at the other slipper. I reached down to grab it, and my fingers brushed the smooth, magical glass, but then the slipper was jerked off my foot. The magic filling me drained away in a flash, and the world went briefly— then permanently—black.

18

When I woke, my head was cushioned on a soft pillow, and a bandage was wrapped around my leg. My feet were bare.

I wiggled my toes and then peeled my eyes open. I was in a medium-sized room with whitewashed walls. A torch filled the room with enough light for me to make out a clothes chest, a wardrobe, and an empty birdcage hanging from a hook. A crooked pile of books leaned against the clothes chest, and a memory flashed through me: Danica with her face buried in a book, as usual.

I couldn't see the slippers, but I could feel them, filling the air with a sharp, wild tingle, making the soles of my feet itch to put them on.

"We have to trust her, Danica!" A door slammed on the other side of the room. I closed my eyes and tried to make my hands go limp. "She came here, didn't she? She left that witch and came to *us*."

"Hush, Esme! You'll wake her."

"I want her to wake," Esme said. "Aren't you excited to finally talk to her?"

"Of course I am," Danica snapped. "I almost drowned trying to get her here. But we have to be careful. She might not be the sister we remember."

My heart was thudding so loud I could hear it. How was it possible they couldn't hear it too?

"For once in your life, Esme, *think*. Who's to say she hasn't fallen for that sweet, loving act Cinderella used to get the prince?" When Danica said *Cinderella*, the first syllable came out in a hiss and the last syllable sounded like she was throwing it against the wall.

"She didn't! She wouldn't! She brought us the slippers, didn't she?" Someone touched my toe, and I burst into giggles.

Oops.

Esme squeaked and jumped back. I opened my eyes, but only halfway. Maybe I could get away with pretending I had been asleep until now. "What did you do that for?" I said groggily. "I'm ticklish."

"Yes," Danica said. "I remember that about you."

I sat up. The side of my leg, where the shark had bitten me, ached with the movement.

My sisters stood side by side, next to the bed. Esme was short with a round, wide-eyed face, and Danica was taller and thinner and sharp-boned. Aside from that, they looked very alike. Narrow, identical curves at the bridges of their noses, prominent chins, eyes set wide apart . . . They looked alike, and they looked familiar.

They looked like me.

Esme grinned at me. Danica watched me coolly, with an expression I couldn't read. Expectancy hung heavily in the air, and I didn't know what, exactly, they expected of me.

"Are you all alone here?" I asked.

Esme and Danica exchanged amused glances. That spurred another memory, of those same condescending looks on younger faces. *Go away, Tirza. You'll understand when you're older.*

"She really did keep a lot from you, didn't she?" Danica asked.

No need to wonder who *she* was. Danica managed to inject that short word with as much loathing as she'd gotten into the four syllables of *Cinderella.*

"We have supporters among the Larosians," Esme said. "They don't like Cinderella either." Esme's voice was softer and more hesitant than Danica's, but she said *Cinderella* with the exact same vitriol. "She's prejudiced against foreigners. Always suspecting people of trying to invade her country, and threatening to use magic against them if they do. The Larosians would much rather see one of us on the throne."

"Where we should have been all along," Danica added.

The reason Cinderella thought the Larosians might invade Tarel was because the Larosians had tried to do exactly that. In fact, they had tried five times over the past twenty years. But I wasn't about to start my reunion with my sisters by arguing about politics.

"We were the ones who were meant to have the slippers," Danica went on. "But *she* stole them from us, and took everything we had worked for, and exiled us to this place where we could not fight back." Her face untwisted, and she smiled at me. "Until now."

"What about my . . . about our . . ."

My voice trailed off. But my sisters knew what I meant.

"Did *she* not tell you what happened to our mother?" Danica asked.

"She told me that Mother died," I said. "But no one ever told me how, so I was never sure. . . ."

"It's true," Esme said gently.

It shouldn't have hurt. I had known for years that my mother was dead. Yet somehow, it felt just like that moment in the castle, long ago, when the queen had first told me the news.

"It's Cinderella's fault," Esme said, and her voice mingled with the memory. I had thought it back then, too, though I had never dared say it aloud. "After all those years of sheltering that stupid girl, keeping her fed and clothed, to have her turn on us like that. . . ."

A new memory floated to the front of my mind: Cinderella on her hands and knees, scrubbing the floor while Danica flicked almond shells onto the freshly cleaned tiles behind her.

"Weren't we . . ." The clearest part of the memory was my own childish laughter. I flinched away from it. "Weren't we . . . kind of mean to her?"

Esme gaped at me like she couldn't believe what I had said. I couldn't quite believe it either. The sudden silence made me want to shiver.

Danica turned, and I saw that the frozen feeling was coming from the ice in her eyes.

"I think," she said, "that you've been listening to too many ballads. Don't forget who paid to have them written."

Actually, the queen hated the songs about her. She wished the minstrel would start obsessing about love or flowers or ancient battles instead.

Or so she had told me. Everything I knew about her, everything I believed about my own family, I had heard from *her*.

"I'm sorry," I said, feeling my face flame. "In the castle, I had to pretend to believe all her lies. I'm not used to being allowed to tell the truth."

"Was there no one you could trust?" Esme asked. "Has she really fooled everyone?"

"Yes," I said. "I mean ... everyone except me."

That part sounded weak, and Danica shot me a sharp glance.

But Esme nodded. "She was good at that, even before she had the slippers to help her. Our own mother was taken in by her at the beginning. But the three of us— we could *always* tell her true nature. Even you, Tirza. You were just a child, but you knew enough to refuse her bribes, and to come tell us whenever she was trying one of her tricks."

"I ... I did?" I asked.

"Oh yes," Danica agreed. "Very often, we would not have known what she was up to if not for you." She smiled at me, and the air in the room thawed noticeably. "All these years in exile, only one thing has kept us going: the knowledge that someday you would rejoin us, and together we would make her pay." She walked over to the clothes chest, opened it, and pulled out the glass slippers. They dangled from her hand, glimmering bright, as if they were drawing every mote of light from the dim room and reflecting them back at us.

My skin tingled, as if that same light was dancing in my blood.

I drew in my breath. The sound whipped through the

small, still room, and I wished I could take it back. But Danica gave me a knowing look, like she understood how I felt and didn't blame me for it.

I couldn't remember the last time anyone had looked at me like that.

"Go ahead," Danica said. She held the slippers out to me. "Put them on."

I swung my legs over the side of the bed. The floor tiles were cold under my bare feet.

"Why did you take the slippers *off* my feet, then?" I asked.

I hated myself for being suspicious, when *they* weren't acting suspicious of me. But the years in the castle couldn't fall away that fast. Nobody had ever liked me, except one person, and that person hadn't really liked me at all. He had just been paid to act like he did. Nobody had ever tried to be nice to me just because I was *me*.

So this is what it's like to have a family, I thought.

"Your leg was covered with blood," Esme explained. "We needed to get the slippers off so we could clean you up."

The cut was on my *leg*, not my foot. Though probably some of the blood had dripped down into my foot . . .

It didn't matter. Danica was still holding the slippers out, and I could feel them calling to me; it was as if the wildness within them had seeped into me, and we could no longer bear to be separated. I crossed the room and reached for them, tensed for a trick, but Danica didn't pull them away. She let me take them.

I didn't need to be suspicious. Not here. I put the slippers on the floor and slipped my feet into them.

A shock ran through me, followed by a burst of exhilaration. It flowed through my body, meeting and mingling with the warmth in my chest. My sisters watched me, smiling.

I had always thought the slippers were astonishingly elegant. The few times I had glimpsed them, I hadn't been able to take my eyes off them. Perhaps some part of me, even then, had known they were mine. But now I could see that their beauty was nothing compared to their power.

These slippers could do anything. Yet all the queen had ever done with them, once she'd gotten what she wanted, was keep them in her closet and put them on for a few hours once a year. How could she not have felt what they were really capable of?

Because they weren't meant for her, I thought. *They were meant for me.*

"Oh, Tirza," Esme breathed. "They fit perfectly!"

"Of course they do," Danica said, but beneath her gruffness I heard a note of pride.

I couldn't tell if it was the slippers or my sisters—or both—but something inside me woke and stretched, expanding past the barriers I had always kept around my heart. It was too fierce and joyful to leave room for suspicion.

And not being suspicious meant I could ask questions, because I could trust the answers.

"I wasn't bleeding on my feet," I said. "Why did you need the slippers to come off in order to fix my leg?"

"The slippers were drawing on your blood," Esme said. "It's harder to heal a cut when there's something pulling the blood out."

"The slippers were *what?*"

"That's where they get their power," Danica explained. "From those with fae blood who wear them." Her eyebrows slanted downward. "Didn't you use your blood to take them in the first place?"

"No. But . . ." I remembered the bite searing into my calf as I thrashed in the ocean, the dizziness as the blood rushed out of me. The surge I had felt from the slippers.

They hadn't been reacting to my terror. They had been reacting, fierce and eager, to my *blood*. It hadn't happened right away, because it must have taken a few seconds for the blood from my calf to reach the slippers.

But I hadn't bled at all when I took them that first

time. I would not have forgotten bleeding on the queen's white carpet.

Danica considered. "If you didn't bleed on them, did you at least dance in them?"

"Yes." The whirling, graceful feeling of twirling around the queen's room, the wildness in my heart leaping to meet the magic in the slippers. "I didn't realize they were taking my, um . . ."

"Your energy," Danica finished. "Dancing is a much weaker source than blood, but I suppose the slippers were desperate. Cinderella was wearing them just once a year, and I'll bet she barely scratched her heel first. Just enough to keep the slippers tied to her, to keep her prince bewitched with her." She laughed. "She's still the mousy little coward she always was. She's too afraid to use the slippers the way they were meant to be used. They're *starved* for power. Can't you feel it?"

Esme was watching me closely. "Slow down, Danica."

It had always been rare for Esme to interrupt Danica. Judging by Danica's expression, it still was. "We don't have time to slow down!"

Esme flushed but persisted. "I don't think Tirza knew any of this. Did you, Tirza?"

"No," I admitted. I wanted them to think that I was smart and loyal, that I had intended all along to rejoin them. But I had decided to trust them, so I might as well go ahead and trust them. "I didn't even know the slippers were magical. Queen—Cind—*she* never told me. She never told me anything."

Esme sighed. "It must have been so terrible for you. We should have sent you messages earlier. But after Mother died, it was ... Things were difficult, and that boy said you were happy, and ..."

She stepped forward suddenly and wrapped me in a hug. Before I could recover from my surprise and hug her back, she let go of me.

"I'm so glad you're here, Tirza," she said. Her voice trembled before she steadied it. "I'm so glad the three of us are together at last."

Danica stood back, eyebrows raised, but not in a scornful manner. I found that I didn't mind. I suspected Danica wasn't the hugging type.

"We knew you would find a way back to us," Danica said, and the confidence in her voice was better than a hug. "Now that the three of us are together, we can start planning to turn the tables on Cinderella."

19

Danica had said, "*We* can start planning." But it quickly became clear that what she meant was *I have planned everything, and the two of you can listen to me explain my plan. At length. With a lot of repetition to make sure you understand every detail.*

Esme sat at the table next to me, completely silent except for the occasional "Mm-hm" and "Oh, yes." She nodded in all the right places, but once, when I glanced over, I caught her with her eyes half shut and a tiny smile on her mouth, like she was daydreaming about something other than Danica's description of how many chains we would wrap around Cinderella's wrists before marching her out to the boat.

Esme, clearly, had heard all this before.

And Danica, clearly, had spent a *lot* of time thinking it through. She also seemed to believe that once we walked into the ball with the slippers, everyone would realize they had been wrong all along. According to her, once the people understood how they had been tricked, they would turn on Cinderella. I didn't think it would be that simple, but I wasn't sure how to tell her that.

Since I couldn't get a word in edgewise, it wasn't much of an issue.

Luckily, we needed a snack while we planned—or at least, so Esme announced, and I wasn't about to contradict her. The snack was muffins that tasted a lot like cupcakes, except without frosting. Which tasted, actually, like Dame Yaffa's cupcakes. According to Danica, Dame Yaffa had been helping them for years, smuggling food and clothes to their Larosian sympathizers farther up the coast and sending them information directly by messenger bird. She was also the one who had suggested that Aden be my friend.

"That he spy on me, you mean?" I muttered, and Esme's mouth turned down.

"We wanted to make sure you were all right, Tirza," she said. "He was helping us."

"Then why did it have to be a secret?"

Danica sighed. I was interrupting her monologue. "You were *seven*, Tirza! We couldn't trust you to keep it quiet. Especially when Cinderella was so good at worming her way into your affections."

"We were worried that we had lost you," Esme said

softly. "Aden said that you had your own room in the royal castle. He told us that Cinderella took you on outings for your birthdays, just the two of you, and that you were always eager to go. He said you wore the colors she recommended and played with her sons. We were pretty sure you were only pretending, but we had to be careful."

"I understand," I said. "The— I mean, Qu— I mean—"

Cinderella. I had always been so careful not to use that name, even in the privacy of my own thoughts. Because if I ever slipped up and said it out loud . . .

All my life, *she* had made sure I was afraid, and I hadn't realized it until now. But I wasn't afraid anymore.

"Cinderella," I said, loudly and defiantly. I managed to get the name out, but it didn't sound like it had when Danica said it. I sounded like a little girl, trusting and hopeful.

Cinderella! Cinderella, will you play cards with me?

I can't, Tirza, I need to finish this mending. . . .

"Cinderella," I said, pushing the memory away, "pretended to be kind, but she never fooled me. None of that was as great as it sounds. My room in the castle . . . It was a very out-of-the-way room. With a view of the Larosian peninsula, to remind me that I could have been sent into exile. And it had mice! The que—Cinderella refused to get rid of them."

"Oh, right." Danica rolled her eyes. "Cinderella and her mice. Remember how she treated them practically like pets?"

"I caught her *feeding* them," Esme said with a shudder.

"At least the squeaky creatures loved her. Nobody else did."

I shifted. The four muffins I had eaten (walking across an ocean takes a *lot* of energy, okay?) were like rocks in my stomach.

The slippers, however, felt smooth and perfect. I couldn't imagine ever taking them off again.

"Time to go," Danica said, pushing her chair back. "This is going to be harder once the tide turns."

"What's going to be harder?" I asked.

"I'll explain on the way," Danica said, and swept out of the cottage while my mouth was still moving.

"I don't doubt you will," I muttered, and Esme laughed aloud. She reached over and gave me a quick, deep hug. Esme, apparently, was into hugs. And probably starved for them, given that it had been just her and Danica for so many years.

"Danica means well," Esme said. "But she also really likes doing things her way. It's best to go along with her."

"Why?" I asked. "What happens if you don't?"

"She gets angry. She would never hurt either of us, but she can be very intense."

"I noticed," I said. "She's more . . . *her* . . . than she used to be, right?"

Esme laughed again, her cheeks turning shiny pink. "It's not her fault. Ever since Mother died, she's been the one taking charge of everything."

"Because she had to?" I asked. "Or because she wanted to?"

Esme blinked, and the mirth disappeared from her face. "You don't understand, Tirza. You haven't been with us all these years in exile. I was so scared of the slippers I would have lived the rest of my life in hiding if I could." She wrapped her arms around herself. "But Danica is brave. She deals with her fear by being . . . herself . . . but at least she deals with it. She does what has to be done. If we get to return from exile and defeat Cinderella, it's going to be entirely because of Danica."

"You didn't say you were afraid of Cinderella," I pointed out. "You said you were afraid of the slippers."

Esme's eyes widened, and she glanced furtively around the cottage, as if worried that Danica had come back. "Of Cinderella wearing the slippers, is what I meant. Obviously."

Before I could respond, she turned and walked out of the cottage.

After a moment, I strode out into the moonlight and broke into a trot until I caught up to my sisters.

Evidently, Aden had left a couple of things out of his reports to my sisters. Like the fact that I was not the kind of person you could lead down a slippery, treacherous path in the dead of night. At least, not if you wanted me to end up on the beach at the bottom of the path instead of plummeting into the ocean.

The shark-infested ocean.

By the time Esme and I caught up to her, Danica had already started down the cliff side. At first, I couldn't understand how she was managing it. Then I got closer and saw a very narrow, very steep set of stairs set into the rock. To anyone who didn't know it was there, it would look like nothing but a faint zigzag.

"I don't think—" I began. But Esme was already descending after Danica, as confidently as if they had both done this a hundred times.

I swallowed hard and followed. The waves below me—far, far below me—blurred into a froth of black-and-white. The steps were so narrow that sometimes I had to turn my feet sideways to make them fit. One little slip, one loss of balance, and there would be nothing to stop me from plunging all the way to the sea.

"Don't look down," Esme called up to me.

Good advice for most people, maybe. But if I didn't watch my feet, I was guaranteed to fall. As opposed to if

I *did* look at my feet, in which case, I was only ninety-five percent likely to fall.

I was halfway down the cliff before it occurred to me that not only had I not tripped and fallen to my death, I hadn't even slipped or lost my balance. And I was keeping up with my sisters without making any extra effort at all.

The slippers, lending me their grace and power.

The surf crashed furiously against the cliff far below, growing louder as we descended. The stairs ended in a very small area of damp sand wedged between shiny black rocks. The ocean was so thunderous that Danica had to raise her voice to be heard. "Let me go over the plan again." Her hair was as black as the rocks behind her, except it glistened in the moonlight. "You understand the basics, right? We—"

"Yes," I said hastily, before she could get started. "We're going to sneak into the ball tomorrow night and prove that the slippers are rightfully ours." A wave broke onto the small beach, and I stepped back from it. I didn't want to argue with my sisters, but . . . "It might not be as easy as you expect. People at the castle don't exactly like me. But they love *her*."

Danica shook her head, letting the froth wash over her feet. "They love her because of the slippers. Without them, she'll lose her power to bewitch people. They'll see clearly that she's been lying to them all along."

"And *you'll* be the one wearing the slippers." Esme looked anxiously from me to Danica. I could almost feel the force of her desire for me to agree. "So everyone will believe *you*."

I knew I should stop talking; it was only making them suspicious of me. And they were the only two people in the world who currently *weren't* suspicious of me. (Well, except for Aden. Who didn't count because *I* was suspicious of *him*.)

I stepped closer to the ocean, then realized the obvious problem.

"There's no boat," I said.

"There's a boat waiting for us near the castle," Danica explained. "While you were asleep, we sent a bird with a message to Dame Yaffa, and she sent a reply. She prepared everything. All you need to do is walk across the ocean and bring the boat to us."

"Oh, is that all?" Another wave lapped onto the sand. "That didn't work out so well last time."

"But this time you bled on the slippers," Danica said. "They've absorbed more than enough power to carry you all the way across."

White lines rose and disappeared on the black water. Tiny shivers ran through me. "Are you sure? I'd really prefer not to be dumped into a shark-infested ocean again."

"There are no sharks in these waters," Danica said.

"Tell that to the one that bit my leg!"

"Those were probably bluefish. Vicious creatures, but not deadly. You could have outswam them if you weren't so panicked."

"The slippers failed the qu—they failed *Cinderella* too." It was getting easier, with practice, to say *Cinderella*. "At that first ball, when they stopped working at midnight."

"Midnight had nothing to do with it," Danica said. "Cinderella was drawing on the slippers' power very heavily the night of the ball—she had to make herself appear regal and beautiful, *and* enchant the prince despite how dull she is. They ran out of power after only a couple of hours." Her lips curled into a smirk. "She should have given them more blood. I suppose she wasn't brave enough for that."

The sea was calmer now, but the waves were still coming—masses of surging water rising and leaping forward before crashing in on themselves. I remembered those waves pulling me under, forcing briny water down my throat.

But my sisters were depending on me. They had been waiting for me, counting on me, all this time. I finally had a chance to prove that I was worth it.

"All right," I said. "If that's what you need me to do, I had better get started."

20

The walk back across the sea was not as fun as the walk to the peninsula had been. I wasn't sure why. Was it because I was anticipating that sudden plunge into the freezing water? Because I was going *back* to the place I had escaped? Because I no longer had a reunion with my sisters to look forward to?

Because I was going back to defeat the queen?

I had plenty of time to try to figure it out as I trudged over the sea. The slippers were clearly working, but somehow, they didn't fill me with the same joyful triumph. Clouds drifted across the dark sky, but they were so thin that the moon shone right through them. This time, I didn't follow the moon's path. Instead, I walked all the way around to the far side of the castle, where, according to Danica, the boat would be waiting for me.

The ocean was calmer now and easier to walk on. The

wind whipped my hair across my face, and I felt very cold and very alone.

Except I'm not alone. For the first time in my life, I'm not alone.

I kept telling myself that as I stepped off the froth onto a strip of sandy beach. Still, it was a great relief when I got to a small wooden rowboat—wedged among some rocks near the shore, as my sisters had promised—and found Aden sleeping in it, both feet propped up on one of the seats, a trail of dribble hanging down from the side of his mouth.

I sat down on the bow seat at the front of the boat and nudged Aden's feet to the side to make room. Quietly, I said, "Hi."

Aden yelped and jumped up, so violently that he dislodged the boat. It slid sideways and toppled over, dumping me into a jumble of small, sharp rocks. An oar hit my shoulder, and I shrieked. Beside me, Aden tumbled with a splat into a shallow pool of seawater.

Startled seagulls fled from us in a commotion of squawks, flapping white wings against the black sky.

"I *told* Jerome the boat wasn't stable," Aden grumbled, sitting up and shaking water off his clothes. "This is his fault! When I get home—"

"Shh!" I hissed, struggling to my feet. "Keep your voice down."

Aden looked at me incredulously. "I think if there's anyone out here, they heard us already."

"They heard crashing and yelling. They don't know it's us. It could have been seagulls."

"Have you ever heard yourself yell? Nobody thought that was a seagull."

"Fine." I picked up the oar, wincing. I'd hit the wound on my calf, and started it hurting all over again. "Let's get out of here, then."

"Yeah." Aden eyed the boat, which was lying on its side. "That's going to be a problem."

It took us five tries to push the boat back over, and then it landed with a thud that sprayed sand all over us. Every creak and rustle on the wind made me jump, expecting soldiers to emerge from the forest that lined the beach. By the time Aden and I braced ourselves on either side of the boat, my muscles were tied in knots.

"Ready," Aden said, "set . . ."

We pushed the boat into the water, then ran into the surf and pulled ourselves in. Inside the boat, I took off the slippers to let my feet dry. It was a wrench to take them off, as if something inside me had drained suddenly away. I realized then that I had never stopped feeling their power. I had just gotten used to it.

The slippers were already dry, smooth and sparkling,

as if they hadn't just dug into sand or been splashed by seawater.

"Um," Aden said. "Are those ..."

"Yes." I folded my hands around the smooth curves of the shoes, touching as much of my skin to them as I could. "But I didn't steal them."

"Uh-huh."

It was unbearable having them off. I slipped them back onto my feet and immediately felt a wave of relief; even the ache in my calf receded. I closed my eyes to savor the feeling. "Just start rowing."

"Why am *I* the one who has to row?"

"We'll take turns," I said. "But since I walked all the way across the ocean while you were taking a nap, I think you should go first."

"It's not called a nap when it's the middle of the night," Aden grumbled. "It's called sleep, and thanks to you, I didn't get much." But he picked up the oars and started rowing.

I didn't actually know how to row, but I figured I would wait to bring that up until Aden said it was my turn.

"So," Aden said as the boat pulled away from the shore. "How are your sisters?"

"You tell me. You're the one who's been working for them all this time."

Aden's gaze flickered sideways. "Are you still mad about that?"

"You've been lying to me for years. How long do you think I should get to be mad about it?"

Aden grunted to remind me how hard he was working at the oars. "I didn't lie. I just didn't mention them. And to be fair, you never asked."

"Being fair is not high on my priority list right now," I snapped. "And what exactly did you think I would ask? 'Hey, Aden, do you want to play Beanstalk, and by the way, are you secretly spying on me for my sisters who were banished from the country years ago?'"

"If you had ever *mentioned* them," Aden said, "I would have told you. But you never did."

I crossed my arms over my chest.

"Okay," Aden said, "I sense that's not going to be my winning argument."

"Do you sense that you don't *have* a winning argument?"

Aden sighed. "I was doing you a favor, Tirza. Thanks to those messages, we're going to free your sisters *and* rescue you *and* punish Cinderella!"

So he was also calling her Cinderella now? For some reason, that annoyed me. What had the queen ever done to him?

Aden went silent as the boat cut through the waves,

maybe because he realized he was in the wrong. Though probably it was because he was concentrating on rowing.

And then, in a surprisingly short amount of time, the cliffs were towering over us.

"Hey." I blinked at Aden. "You never asked me to take my turn!"

"Yeah, well. Maybe I do owe you." He shrugged between strokes. "Besides, you're probably terrible at rowing."

"That's not true," I said. "I don't know how to row at all."

Aden snickered. Then his face grew serious. "I really am sorry, Tirza. I asked Dame Yaffa a bunch of times if I could explain everything to you, and she always said no. I thought—"

"We have to tell her!" Esme shouted. Her voice sounded as if it was right next to me.

I startled. We were still too far away to see my sisters, but the sea wind carried their voices right to us.

"You always do this." Danica was also yelling. Clearly, my sisters didn't realize how far sound traveled over the water. Aden stopped rowing, and we both sat perfectly still. "I'm not going to change the plan every time someone smiles at you or frightens you or, I don't know, *breathes* on you."

"I'm not trying to change the plan! I just think Tirza should know the truth."

"Of course you do." Danica's sigh mingled with the rush of the waves. "That's why you should leave the thinking to me. I want to trust Tirza as much as you do. But if we tell her how our mother—"

The current carried our boat past the cliff's outcropping, and my sisters came into view, still on the beach where I had left them. They abruptly stopped talking. I stared at the shallow water sloshing in the bottom of the boat, not sure what expression they would see on my face.

"You made it!" Esme said happily. "I mean, not that I thought you wouldn't. We knew you would. But it's so great that you actually did—"

"Keep rowing," Danica interrupted her.

Aden obeyed. When we got close enough, Danica lifted her skirt and stepped into the boat, balancing with apparent ease and settling in the stern seat in the back. Esme grabbed the side of the boat and pulled herself into it in a flurry of hair and skirts. The boat rocked wildly, and Aden struggled to steady it.

Danica laced her fingers neatly over one knee. "Good job, Aden—you are Aden, I assume?" She didn't wait for his nod. "Let's go."

The boat sat a lot lower in the water now, and moved a lot slower when Aden picked up the oars and started to row. No one offered to take over for him. No one said anything at all. Danica and Esme sat together in the stern of the boat: Danica motionless as a statue; Esme twisting her fingers together. Aden rowed steadily, his face shiny with sweat. I sat in the front, in the bow seat, which unfortunately meant I was facing the other three. This made me feel the full impact of the awkward silence.

As the cliffs receded, I tried to think of something to say:

What is it that you're not telling me? Tell me the truth, RIGHT NOW!

So, I guess we all sort of know each other, right?

Do you want to sing a song? The faeries in the forest, they wave their wands, hoorah, hoorah. . . .

Not surprisingly, I didn't actually say any of them.

The current caught the boat and turned it sideways. Aden struggled with the oars, and Esme cleared her throat. "It's really nice weather for a boat ride, isn't it?"

Which only made me happier that I hadn't spoken. Nobody responded, and Esme turned brick red.

Then Danica spoke. Somehow, *her* voice sounded cool and natural, not awkward at all. "Thank you, Tirza. It was brave of you to walk back across the water. Just like it was brave of you to steal those slippers and come find us in the first place."

I straightened.

"You think I stole the slippers?" I repeated.

"We're very proud of you."

"So," I said, "*you* didn't steal them?"

Danica gave me a long look, like she was reconsidering how proud of me she should be. "How could *we* have stolen them? We were stuck in Larosia!"

"You could have asked Aden to . . ." Even as I said it, I realized how ridiculous the idea was. I had been carrying it around half formed in the back of my mind, but if I had ever pulled it out and examined it, I would have seen at once that it was impossible. My sisters had been trapped across the ocean. Aden would never dare enter the queen's room. Dame Yaffa hadn't stepped foot in the castle in at least six years.

I still didn't know who had stolen the slippers. Or why.

I cleared my throat. But just then, Aden gasped.

The boat had turned around completely, so I couldn't see the castle or beach getting closer. All I could see was the Larosian cliffs getting smaller and less distinct, until they looked almost exactly like the view from my window. So I didn't know at first why Aden's brow furrowed or why that same sight made Danica smile.

"That's not the plan," Aden said. "She was supposed to meet us in the village!"

I twisted around to see what they were staring at.

We were closer to shore than I had realized. The castle loomed against the sky, above a dark strip of beach rimmed with white froth. And on the beach, waiting with her arms crossed over her chest, stood Dame Yaffa.

21

As soon as the boat got close to the beach, Aden and I leapt out and pulled it in. Esme and Danica sat in the boat until they were able to step out onto dry land—well, damp sand—and then Esme scurried over to stand next to me. Danica remained next to the boat, the breeze whipping her hair away from her face.

"We have a problem," Dame Yaffa said.

Esme's fingers dug into my wrist. "That doesn't sound good."

"Well, no," Danica said. "That's generally what it means when people say there's a problem."

Esme flushed, and Dame Yaffa laughed. "I see the two of you haven't changed."

"You are wrong," Danica said. "We have changed a great deal."

Dame Yaffa's smile vanished. "I'm sorry. I know how hard it has been for you. I would have come for you earlier, but Cinderella was careful. She knows that the slippers aren't my only source of magic. She never let me get near the castle, and she kept Tirza on a very short leash."

"We're here now," Danica said. "That's all that matters. What is the problem?"

Esme was clinging to my hand so hard it was starting to hurt. I thought about twisting free, but I kind of liked it, despite the pain.

"We're too exposed here," Dame Yaffa said. "Follow me."

She turned and headed up the beach toward the woods. Danica strode after her, and the rest of us followed. Esme let go of my hand, and sand slid under my feet as I struggled to keep up. The slippers weren't making it easier to walk on the sand, and I wondered if that meant they had used up the power from my blood.

And if so, what I would be expected to do about it.

Then again, I managed to make it all the way into the woods without tripping over an exposed root or stumbling on any rocks. So I suspected the slippers had some magic left.

"It's Cinderella," Dame Yaffa said, coming to a stop in a small clearing. The trees arched darkly over us, their branches blocking most of the moonlight. The forest was filled with rustling and murmurs. "She's planning to follow Tirza to Larosia."

Danica made a strangled sound.

"She's made secret arrangements to row across in the morning while everyone is distracted by preparations for the ball. Even the king doesn't know. She's taking only two trusted guards with her." Dame Yaffa smirked. "Luckily, one of those guards has loved my cupcakes since he was a child."

I can't trust anyone in this castle, the queen had said to me. I pushed away a surge of sympathy for her. "What is she planning?" I asked.

"Isn't it obvious?" Dame Yaffa said. "She needs to get the slippers back before the ball tomorrow night." She leaned back against a gnarled tree trunk. "She doesn't know she can call them, so she has no choice but to go after them. But once she gets to the peninsula, she'll realize that all *three* of you are gone, and then we'll have lost the chance to take her by surprise. So we have to go to the castle now."

All three of you. The phrase sent a sweet, thrilling hum through my body, even as *Go to the castle now* made me want to throw up.

"No," Danica said. "We wait for tomorrow night. We have to unmask her at the ball, in front of everyone."

"That's no longer—"

"Who goes there?" a male voice shouted, and Dame Yaffa stopped talking. The voice came from the direction of the castle.

Aden was the first to move. He took off, racing from the clearing deeper into the woods.

The rest of us immediately decided that he had the right idea. We crashed through the underbrush after him. Branches whipped at my legs. A root came up hard against my ankle, and for a terrifying moment, I thought I had sprained it. But warmth surged from the slippers, and the pain receded as fast as if it had never been. I realized that my calf had stopped hurting too.

"Should we separate?" I gasped as we ran. I knew from playing in these woods with Aden that voices carried deceptively here; the guard was still near the castle—not as close as he had sounded. But that also meant *we* were making enough noise for him to easily track us. "That way he won't catch all of us."

"He won't catch any of us." Dame Yaffa came to a stop, and I slammed into her back. Esme, who had been right behind me, grabbed my shoulders to steady herself. "Tirza, you need to use the slippers."

In the distance, twigs cracked and snapped, and the guard swore. Despite the branches crisscrossing the sky, the moon gave enough light for me to see Dame Yaffa's taut jaw and narrowed eyes.

And the knife she had drawn from somewhere within her clothes. She held it out to me, hilt first.

Something wild and surprising stirred in my blood,

something that thrilled but also scared me. A part of me *wanted* to take that knife, to let my blood flow into the slippers and feel their magic wash through me. All that power, just waiting.

You can't trust the way they make you feel, the queen's voice whispered in my mind.

I stepped back, unable to separate all the different impulses swirling through me. "I'm not sure . . . I think they're dangerous."

"Who told you that?" Danica sneered. "Cinderella?"

I opened my mouth, but then closed it. Because of course, it had been Cinderella.

The knife was steady and waiting in Dame Yaffa's hand. The silence stretched, interrupted only by cracks and rustles as the guard got closer. It sounded like he was trying to be stealthier, which also meant he was moving slower . . . but still, we didn't have much time to waste.

The slippers' power surged through me, *wanting*, but my hand remained clenched at my side.

"I can't," I said. "I'm sorry."

Danica stepped back, her eyes wide and dark. "Then how are you planning to help us?" she demanded. "Or do you want us to get caught?"

"Tirza, please," Esme said. "This is how things are supposed to be. Don't betray us now."

"I'm not!" Behind us, the guard was getting closer. "I

don't need to use the slippers. Not yet. I'll go toward the guard, and once he sees me, I'll be the one he follows. He doesn't even know who the rest of you are. While I draw him off, you can get safely to the village."

"What about you?" Esme asked.

"I'll be punished." I swallowed hard. "But not as badly as you would be."

I reached down and pulled one slipper from my foot. It came off with a tearing sort of pain, an ache deep inside me, as if the slipper had taken part of my soul with it. I gritted my teeth, pulled off the other slipper, and stepped down on a sharp pebble. I yelped and hopped up, grabbing my foot in one hand.

The actual physical pain was a nice distraction from the anguish of removing the slippers. "Here," I managed to say, and held them out. "Take them with you, so the—so Cinderella can't get them back. I'll tell her I lost them in the ocean."

The pain also helped me get the inflection of *Cinderella* almost right. Esme blinked at me, then reached out and took the slippers.

"But you're the only one who can wear them," she said.

A tree branch fell with a *crack*, and the guard swore again. Twigs snapped as he moved closer.

"Once you're safe," I said, "send Aden back with them."

I turned to Aden. He was staring at me wide-eyed. "Hide them in a clothes chest or something. Someplace where I'll be able to get them before the ball."

"Right," Aden said, his voice high-pitched. "Um. How will you know which clothes chest they're in?"

"Don't worry about that," I said. "I'll feel them." I could feel them now, and it was all I could do not to snatch them back out of Esme's hands. "Then we'll go ahead with the original plan. Just like you wanted, Danica."

Esme looked down at the slippers with a sort of wonder mixed with longing—an expression I would have found strange if I didn't recognize it so well. "Are you sure, Tirza? You don't know what Cinderella might do to you."

No. I'm not sure. Give them back.

My stomach clenched. I forced myself to look away from the slippers. "If she throws me in the dungeon," I said, "you'll just have to get me out. Again."

Because I wasn't watching her, I had no warning that Esme was moving. Suddenly, her arms tightened around me.

"We have to go," Dame Yaffa said, and Esme stepped away.

"Take care," Danica said. "Don't do something stupid and get yourself executed before we can rescue you."

Which, I suspected, was Danica's version of a hug.

"Don't worry," I said, and almost added: *The queen wouldn't execute me.* But that would have seriously ruined the moment. So instead, I said, "But also, don't take too long."

"We won't," Danica promised. "By the end of tomorrow, we'll be together again."

"Wait," Aden said. "Tirza, I'm not sure you should—"

"Don't move!" the guard yelled, and he sounded *extremely* close.

"Go!" I said, and they all turned and ran.

Why did I always expect people to argue when I tried to be self-sacrificing?

The guard crashed through the trees. "Stay where you are!" he shouted. "Or I'll cut you down before you can take a single step!"

I turned.

I didn't recognize this guard, but he clearly recognized me. His expression changed swiftly from anger to contempt.

"You!" he said.

"Me," I agreed.

I barely had time to see him draw his sword before he was swinging it in a long, deadly arc at my throat.

22

"No!" I cried. "Wait! The queen wants me alive!"

His blade stopped an inch from my neck. (Impressive swordsmanship. Not that I was in the mood to appreciate it.) His eyes snapped to my bare feet and then back to my face. "How did you get out here?"

"It's a long story," I said.

The sword's edge moved closer to my skin.

"And one the queen will want to hear," I added hastily, stepping back. My foot came down on something wet and mushy and probably very gross. "You should bring me to her. Unharmed."

I tried hard not to look afraid, and tried even harder not to think about what I was stepping in. Whatever it was, it was now oozing up between my toes.

Finally, the guard sheathed his sword with a hiss of steel. He moved beside me to take my arm, and his booted foot plunked next to my bare feet, sending wet chunks flying up to land on my leg. He looked down at what he had stepped in and recoiled.

"Get moving," he muttered, and yanked me sideways.

Being pulled barefoot over rough ground by an impatient guard (probably in a rush to clean off his boots) was extremely unpleasant. The forest floor was covered with sharp stones, rough roots, and large patches of sucking mud. By the time we reached the castle gates, my feet hurt in a dozen places, my arms and legs were thoroughly scratched up, and I had clearly stepped in far grosser things than whatever was sliming up the guard's boots. It was too dark to see my feet, but I could smell them.

Another guard stood at the entrance to the castle. When he saw me, his eyes widened.

"What is she doing back?" he demanded.

"Something wicked, no doubt," the first guard drawled. "Get someone to return her to the dungeon, will you? I've got to get back on patrol."

I waited until the first guard crashed away through the underbrush (honestly, what was the point of patrolling if you were going to be so noisy about it?) and then looked at the new guard. I recognized him. He was the guard who had been outside my door that first night—the one Aden had successfully bribed.

The guard in the forest had said, *How did you get* out?

By which he meant, *out of the castle,* because he thought he had caught me in the act of escaping. But this guard had said, *What is she doing* back?

He knew I had already escaped. Which meant *he* was one of the guards Queen Ella had trusted with her plan. And he was probably the one who had betrayed her and told Dame Yaffa about it.

Which should mean he was on my side. But the way he was scowling at me ... It didn't feel like he was on my side.

"I'm glad you're here," I said, trying to sound confident. "This is all part of Dame Yaffa's plan." I paused, but he didn't react with shock. Which meant he *was* the guard who had betrayed the queen. "I need you to bring me directly to Queen Ella."

"Oh," he snorted. "Is that what you need?"

Buy their loyalty, Aden had said. This guard had turned traitor for money. And I didn't exactly have any on me.

But *he* didn't know that.

I lowered my voice. "For extra pay, of course."

His next snort was even more amused than his first one. "Really. Where are you hiding your coin? Under the mud?"

Okay, so maybe he did know that.

"I don't have coin on me," I said. "Obviously. I wasn't trying to pretend I did. I mean, that would be ridiculous."

He didn't snort this time, but a snort was implied.

"Dame Yaffa will pay you—"

Oh. He had just been saving up for an extra-loud snort. "She still hasn't paid me for letting you escape the first time." He grabbed my arm and pulled me into the castle.

Perfect, I told myself. *I want to be captured.* But when he stopped at the door leading down to the dungeon, I yanked back so fast that I almost slipped through his grip.

"You're not supposed to send me there," I said, trying to keep panic out of my voice. "The queen doesn't want me in the dungeon, because—" My mind went blank.

The guard sighed. Amazingly, his sigh was nearly as derisive as his snorts. "I'll put you in your room for now. But I don't doubt that I'll be transferring you to the dungeon very soon."

I didn't doubt it either. But *very soon* seemed preferable to *right this second.*

When we reached my room, the guard kicked the door open and shoved me inside so hard I fell. Startled mice skittered against the walls.

I waited on my hands and knees, braced for whatever he would say next. But all I heard was the slam of the door and the click of the lock.

"Oh, come on," I said. "Not even a goodbye snort?"

My voice came out shakier than I would have liked. Not that it mattered. No one but the mice could hear me.

I got to my feet. I had left a smear of brown sludge on the rug, which bothered me. That was silly—no matter how things went tomorrow, this wouldn't be my room for long—but I had always loved that rug. It had white-and-pink patterns swirled with blue and gray, like a permanent sunrise. The queen had bought it for me when I was six years old.

A gift, I had thought then. Something else I had to be grateful for. But in truth, it had been less than nothing, compared to what she had stolen from me.

The lock on my door clicked open. I whirled, wishing I had spent my few seconds of solitude cleaning myself up—as much as possible, anyhow. Since it was too late for that, I drew myself upright and did my best to look haughty.

The door swung open, and I let out an involuntary gasp.

I had been prepared—sort of—to face Cinderella. She might be angry enough to throw me into the dungeon, but she wouldn't really hurt me. She wouldn't *kill* me.

I had no such certainty to back me up now. I stepped back, thinking seriously about running again. But my heel hit the bed, a reminder that I had nowhere to run *to*.

"Well, now," said King Ciaran. "Look who we have here."

23

The king crossed his arms over his chest. He was wearing ordinary clothes—ordinary for a king, anyhow: a white silk tunic and a dark gray velvet cape. But it didn't really matter what he was wearing. He was the kind of person who would have looked regal and intimidating in rags.

I sat down on my bed with a thump. The plush mattress sank beneath me, and too late, I realized I'd gotten my blanket dirty too.

"So," King Ciaran said, closing the door behind him. "What should we do with you?"

He didn't say it in a cackling-villain kind of way. He said it like he was genuinely interested in my opinion.

I was pretty sure he wasn't. Still, it was worth a try. "You should probably ask your wife. I don't think she would be very happy if you killed me without consulting her first."

Despite my attempt to sound brave, my voice shook.

"I appreciate your concern for my marital happiness." King Ciaran walked over to the bed and sat, far too close to me. I sidled away, very aware that *I* was the kind of person who couldn't manage to look intimidating in a full ball gown, much less when I was barefoot and covered with mud. "But *you*, Tirza, have always been the biggest problem in my marriage. My wife's blindness about you is incredibly frustrating. Even now, she's angry at me for putting you in the dungeon. Of course, I'm angry at her for preventing me from shooting you when you fled." He crossed his arms over his chest. "Why did you come back, Tirza?"

"I changed my mind," I said. "I want to make amends."

He clearly didn't believe me, but just as clearly, he didn't really care. "Where are the slippers?"

"I lost them." I swallowed hard. "In the ocean."

His face was so still he might have been a statue, if not for the purple shadows under his eyes and the grizzle covering his face. He wasn't wearing a gold band around his head, and his hair fell over his eyes in an unkempt straggle. I forced myself not to move farther away from him.

"I want to see the queen," I said. "And I'm sure..." My voice wobbled again. I pushed on. "I'm sure she wants to see me."

"Of course she will. She's going to believe your lies, and you're going to break her heart. Again." The king's jaw clenched. "Even when she accepted that you stole her slippers, she couldn't accept that you had done it to hurt her."

"I *didn't*—"

"Oh, enough of that," the king said. "I know you didn't steal them."

My protest died in a strangled gurgle.

King Ciaran leaned back on his hands. On anyone else, that would have looked comfortable; instead I felt like he was coiled to pounce. "You must have realized by now the true importance of the slippers. There's a reason I once spent so much time searching for a woman who could wear them."

A woman. Not *the* woman.

The story we had all been told was that the king had used the slipper to find Cinderella. But that was obviously ridiculous. He couldn't have thought that tall, lanky Danica or short, plump Esme was the woman he'd danced with at the ball.

But he had let them try on the slipper. Them and hundreds of other women whom he must have known weren't Cinderella.

"Because the slippers can only be worn by someone fae," I said. "And the kingdom needs a fae queen."

He nodded.

"That's why you married her?" I asked. "Just because she's fae?"

The king brushed his hair out of his eyes. "For the past six years, you believed I married her because she looked pretty and danced well. Why is that better?"

The truth was that for the past six years, I hadn't thought much about it. I had done my best not to remember how Cinderella had triumphed over my family.

But now that I *was* thinking about it—and now that I had heard the other side of the story—it was obvious how she had done it.

"*That's* why the queen left the slipper behind," I said. "So you would know she was fae. That was why you searched the kingdom for her." This story was a lot less romantic than the one the minstrel told. "You wanted the royal family to have magic again."

"The royal family *needs* to have magic again," the king said. "We are a poor, small country with few natural resources. Without magic, we have no chance of defending ourselves against those who would take what little we have." He straightened. "I had hoped that a fae queen would be able to bring the magic back and demonstrate to the other kingdoms that we are still a force to be reckoned with. But my wife's fae blood is weaker than

I thought. She cannot use the power of the slippers for anything except dancing."

That's what she told you, I thought.

What I said was "So now you regret marrying her?"

"Of course not." Something caught and softened in the king's voice. "I do love her now. We have two children. And maybe one of them . . ." He stopped short, as if realizing he had said too much.

I stared at him.

We have two children.

The royal family needs to have magic again.

You keep sneaking into your mother's room, Gilma had said, on that morning that seemed so distant but had actually only been a few days ago.

"Maybe one of your children," I said slowly, "will inherit her magic and be able to *use* it. That's what you were hoping for, wasn't it?" I stood. "That's why you put the slippers out on the bed. So Baro would find them when he sneaked into your room."

I didn't get punished when I tried to take them.

"That was the plan," the king said. "But you came along first."

"And you decided to let everyone think *I* stole them?" My voice rose.

"I thought you *had* stolen them. The fact that you took

them from the bed instead of the box doesn't change the fact that you took them."

"I didn't take them!"

"Yes," the king said thoughtfully. "I believe you now. I can't see how you would have put them in the boat, if you were the one who took them."

"Why didn't you believe me *then*? Why didn't *anyone* believe me?" I realized, to my horror, that I was about to burst into tears. I turned and walked toward the window so the king wouldn't see my face. "Why did everyone assume I was guilty? Just because of my family, because they think wickedness is in my blood...."

"Don't be silly," the king said. "It wasn't because of your family. It was because of *you*."

"What have I ever done?" Tears slid down my cheeks. One hit the side of my mouth; I licked it off and tasted salt. "I've never hurt the queen!"

"You hate her," King Ciaran said. "You've always hated her."

Outside the window, the sky was growing lighter. The cliffs looked just as they always had, the sea dashing furiously against them. "I—"

"Everyone at court can see it." I heard the king walk across the room toward me. "Everyone but Ella. That's why we believed you were guilty, Tirza. Because we could see that you hated her." He stopped a few feet away from me and added, "For no reason at all."

I had been about to say, *I don't hate her,* but found myself switching in midsentence to *I had reasons.* The result was an inarticulate garble, which was probably just as well.

"Do you remember," King Ciaran said, "what you were doing the first time we met?"

I remembered it well. The vast, silent throne room. The sneers of the nobles as I walked between them. The coldness of the king's gaze, like I was an insect he wanted to flick off his arm.

"Of course I remember," I said. "I was bowing. To you."

"The time before that," the king said. "The second time I came to your house."

I turned around and stared at him.

"The first time I was there, I didn't see you at all. That was when I was searching for the girl who had worn the slippers, when your sisters tried to fool me into thinking it was one of them, and when your mother . . ." He hesitated, then went on grimly. "When your mother died. The second time was weeks later, after the mourning period for your mother was over. Ella insisted on staying with you in the cottage until then, and on delaying your sisters' trials. It was the longest month of my life, but when it was over, I came to your house to bring Ella to our wedding. Don't you remember that day?"

I looked at him blankly.

"I see that you don't." He smiled thinly. "You were spilling glue into Ella's bag, to ruin her clothes."

"I was not!" I said.

"Oh yes, you were. When you were caught, you said you only did it because your sisters forced you to. But I never believed that. Your sisters must have known that once Ella reached the castle, all her clothes would be thrown out and replaced with finer ones. The glue was *your* idea."

"It wasn't!" Something queasy sank into my gut, a now-familiar feeling: that of being accused of something I was almost, but not completely, sure I hadn't done.

King Ciaran's jaw clenched. "Ella told me that you were grief-stricken for your mother, that we had to be patient with you. But it wasn't exactly the first time you played a nasty trick on her, was it? You were her friend when it was just the two of you, but when your sisters tormented her, you liked to be on their side. The three of you made her life miserable."

"If that's true," I snapped, "why didn't she exile me with them?"

"Believe me, I asked her exactly that question." King Ciaran's smile was like a baring of teeth. "She said that you loved her. That you were the only one in that house who loved her. That you were a child being influenced by your sisters, but if we took you under our care, you would not turn out like them."

He paused, waiting for me to say something. But my mouth was so dry that I couldn't have managed to speak, even if I'd had anything to say.

"I always knew she was wrong. You learned to hate her when you were a baby, and you don't just grow out of that sort of belief." His eyes were flinty, and I had to force myself not to look away. "It was no surprise to me when I learned that you had joined with your sisters to attack her. You *do* have their wickedness in your heart. They taught you what to believe when you were too young to even know you were being taught."

"I'm older now," I said, my heart hammering against my ribs.

"And what a difference that's made." He shook his head. "How can you fight the wickedness that's in you if you won't even admit it's there?"

When it became clear that I had nothing to say, he turned and left the room, closing the door and clicking the lock shut behind him.

24

My mother slid the slipper onto my foot, then smiled down at me, the corners of her eyes crinkling. I stretched my leg out, watching the slipper sparkle, happiness welling up within me. I had made my mother proud.

Then my mother's eyes narrowed. "Cinderella!" she shouted, and relief and guilt swept through me as she turned, because she wasn't angry at me. "Those aren't yours! Give them back!"

"No, Mama!" I said. "She doesn't have them, I do! Look—"

I lifted my foot, but the slipper had turned red as fire, scorching the skin of my feet.

"Mama!" This time I screamed it. But my mother was gone. It was Cinderella looking down at me, her eyes ringed with ashes, a black-and-purple bruise coloring her right cheek.

"I missed you," she said.

◆

I sat up in bed, gasping, my skin slick with sweat.

Sunlight streamed in through the window, and the air was hot and stuffy. I must have fallen asleep. The last thing I remembered was pacing back and forth along the length of the room, listening to the scuttling of the mice and trying to figure out what to do next.

I hadn't come up with anything, and now the sky outside my window was streaked with gray, the clouds darkening toward sunset. I had slept nearly the entire day.

I swung my legs over the side of the bed, and flakes of mud fell out of my hair and landed on my shoulder. Everything—my hair, my clothes, the sludge still caking my skin—felt hot and sticky. I blinked, trying to shake off my grogginess. My sisters would be on their way to the ball by now, expecting me to meet them with the slippers.

Hide them in a clothes chest, I had told Aden. I didn't feel the slippers, and there was no way Aden could have gotten them into my room. . . . But just in case, I crossed to my clothes chest and opened it.

No slippers. But a folded pile of silky blue fabric lay on top of my clothes. I pulled it up, and a beautiful blue dress dangled from my hands, decorated with a sparse, delicate pattern of sequins and beads.

I had a dress made for you. She had been telling the truth.

And I wondered suddenly if she had always known that blue was my favorite color. Maybe it wasn't coincidental that my room was painted blue.

One that matches mine.

I let the dress drop back into the chest, went to the washbasin on the other side of the room, and used some of my scented towels to clean the mud and sludge from my skin. When my sisters and I returned in triumph, it would be a historic moment. I didn't want to be filthy and stinking while we did it.

Among other things, I could imagine what the minstrel would do with that.

Actually, I couldn't. What kind of song would she write about tonight's ball? Would she go into exile with the qu—with Cinderella and write a tragic lament about betrayal and revenge? Or would she stay in the castle, keep her position and her room and her dresses, and write an inspiring ballad? *The Stepsisters' Justice,* she might call it, or *The Shoe's on the Other Foot,* or maybe *The Evil Queen* ...

My stomach twisted, and I decided to stop thinking. I concentrated entirely on scrubbing myself clean. When I was done (it took a *lot* of scrubbing), I went back to the clothes chest and reached down to touch the dress.

Cinderella's voice whispered in my mind. *I never thought I was giving up you.*

When I was with my sisters, everything had seemed

clear. But here in the castle, in the room the queen had decorated for me, with the gown she'd had made for me ...

They're bribes, I reminded myself. *You don't owe her anything. This is just a fraction of what she stole from you.*

I shook the dress out and put it on. Unfortunately, it was the kind of dress that required a maid to tighten the sashes. I did my best on my own, but my best wasn't very good. The dress hung on me like a sack.

It would have to do. When I rejoined my sisters, maybe we would have time to tighten my sashes before we overthrew the kingdom.

I found a pair of new satin shoes inside the clothes chest. They matched the dress, so Cinderella must have bought them for me too. They fit perfectly, but they felt heavy and awkward ... almost deliberately so, like a taunt: These *shoes will make you even* less *graceful!* I walked to the door and knocked.

It opened immediately. The guard outside was the same one who had brought me to my room, and apparently, he had not moved since then. He put his hand on his sword hilt.

"What do you think you're doing?" he said.

"Leaving," I replied.

"Right. Find some gold coins in your room, did you?"

"No. I don't have any money." I smiled as confidently as I could. "But that might change by the end of tonight."

He considered that. "Did you really manage to steal the queen's glass slippers?"

I drew in my breath. "Yes," I said. "I did."

He took his hand off his sword hilt. He leaned back against the wall and stared straight ahead, as if he couldn't see me.

He didn't make a sound when I slipped past him and down the stairs.

———◆———

I had been right not to worry about finding the slippers. As soon as I left my room, I felt that wild stirring under my skin, and I didn't even have to think about which way to go. My feet led me down the hall without requiring any direction from my mind, and the sense of power grew stronger with every step I took.

I *did* have to think about not getting caught. Luckily, this close to the ball, most people were in their rooms getting ready. But guards still patrolled the castle, and the occasional noble rushed frantically through the halls to mend a ripped cape or get an opinion about jewelry. Twice I was forced to dodge into a spare room, and once I had to flatten myself behind a window curtain while two noblemen engaged in an extremely long discussion about whether a green tunic could be paired with a navy cape.

All the while I could feel the slippers calling, calling, making my heart pound and my blood sing. I couldn't wait to put them on. Then I wouldn't have to hide and skulk and be ashamed, not ever again.

"Tirza!" a familiar voice squealed, and I whirled.

Baro poked his head out of a doorway and grinned at me, a smear of chocolate on his cheek. "You look pretty!" he said, clapping his hands together.

"Baro! What are you doing here?" I whispered. "You should be in the nursery!"

"I hid the slippers," Baro said proudly.

"You *what?*"

"Like Aden said I should."

I was going to *kill* Aden.

"I'll show you where I put them!" Baro added.

"That's all right. I don't need you to." His smile faded, and I added hastily, "But you did a great job! You'll definitely get a present. Now go back to the nursery, quick, before we ruin the—um—the surprise."

"I'm going with you," Baro said. "Aden said that if I hid the slippers, I could go to the ball."

I wasn't just going to kill Aden. I was going to torture him first.

"Aden made a mistake," I said. "You can't go to the ball. Not this year. But—"

I wasn't sure how I was going to finish that

sentence—my only two ideas were "But you can have candy" and "But you can go next year," neither of which was likely to work. I didn't have to choose, because Baro immediately burst into tears.

"WHY? WHY CAN'T I? IT'S NOT FAIR!"

"Baro, be quiet!" I had seen a maid pass by a minute ago. "You'll get us in trouble."

"I WANT TO GO TO THE *BALL*!"

"It's too dangerous—" I faltered to a stop. The next words out of my mouth were going to be *You're too young.* I had heard these exact excuses a dozen times before.

I had never believed the queen, and Baro was not going to believe me.

But this ball *was* going to be dangerous. More importantly, Baro could not be there to see his mother's defeat.

I dropped to my knees, grabbed Baro, and pulled him into a tight hug. He responded by kicking me in the shins.

"I'll take care of you," I whispered. "I promise. No matter what happens, I'll make sure you're safe."

Baro tangled his fingers in my hair and pulled. I yelped.

"Don't tell anyone you saw me, all right?" I could hear footsteps thudding down the hallway. Probably the maid I had seen earlier. "Be good, and I'll bring you cookies from the ball."

Which was almost as stupid as the promises I had managed *not* to make. What if Cinderella managed to turn the tables again, just like she had six years ago when she stole the slippers from my family and enchanted the prince? What if I ended up in exile—or worse?

I would never see Baro again.

I watched tears roll in huge drops down his cheeks, and I thought about not moving. About waiting here, getting caught, being dragged back to my room and locked inside while the ball went on without me. My sisters, once they realized I had been captured, would go back to the village. They would be furious, but they would still be free. I would be punished, but I would be safe. I would be in this castle, still trapped and scorned and hated, but I would have Baro and Elrin . . . and Aden, if I could ever trust him again. And maybe, just maybe, the queen and I could . . .

The footsteps got closer. With them came the rustle of silk petticoats, and a familiar voice shouted, "Baro! You're supposed to be in bed! I'm going to be late to the ball!"

That wasn't a maid. It was Gilma.

"Don't tell!" I whispered. "It's very important."

Then I let go of him and ran down the hall.

25

The call of the slippers was unmistakable now. It led me down the corridor, around a turn, and straight to a plain bedroom door. When I put my hand on the doorknob, I doubled over from the sizzle that ran all through my body.

The slippers were clearly a lot more powerful than they had been the first time I felt them calling to me, when they had been sitting neatly side by side on the queen's bed. Then, I hadn't been able to tell the feeling was coming from them rather than from myself. Now, the slippers pulled me toward them with a force so strong it was almost physical.

The slippers hadn't felt this powerful in my sisters' cottage or in the woods. Something had happened between last night and now to increase their power.

I remembered Dame Yaffa's knife flashing in the

moonlight and wondered which of my sisters had given the slippers her blood.

I stood with my hand on the doorknob for longer than I should have. Thinking of the fierceness on Danica's face, but also of the confidence with which she had handed me the slippers in their cottage. Remembering Esme's expression in the woods when I had refused to take Dame Yaffa's knife.

I opened the door and stepped into the room. It was an ordinary noblewoman's bedchamber—small (so about twice the size of my bedroom) and neat. The window at the far end of the room was open, which was unusual; most noblewomen kept their windows tightly shut during the day to keep out the heat. The breeze that wafted in was humid, mingled with an oddly metallic scent.

The clothes chest against the wall was wide open. Baro *really* wasn't good at hiding things.

I closed the door and headed across the room, toward the clothes chest. I was halfway there when I stopped.

I never thought I was giving up you.

I had never really thought about giving up *her* either. For all these years, despite my anger, some part of me had believed the queen loved me. That she was trying to protect me.

It wasn't too late to stop this. I could go back to my

room and wait for the queen to come. She would tie my sashes properly, and we would go to the ball together.

I half turned toward the door, but the longing for the slippers went through me like a shock. I turned again and took another step toward the chest.

Behind me, the door creaked open.

I whirled, my heart pounding. Then I let out a breath of relief. "Aden!"

Aden slipped into the room and closed the door behind him. "I came to warn you: This isn't a safe place to hide. Baro spilled a drink, and now there's a spot of juice on Gilma's glove. She's already dressed for the ball, so she's acting like it's a national crisis. As soon as she gets him into bed, she's going to come here to replace her gloves."

"Gilma?" I blinked. "This is *her* room? Why would you hide the slippers in *Gilma's* room?"

"It wasn't my idea," Aden said defensively.

"But it *was* your idea to give this very important job to a five-year-old, right? What were you thinking?"

"I was *thinking*," Aden retorted, "that he's the only person in the castle who wouldn't be searched, but who would keep a secret for you. And who wouldn't be in danger of being executed if he got caught."

Oh. Actually, that was pretty good thinking.

"Thank you," I said grudgingly. I started toward the chest, then stopped again, caught by the expression on Aden's face. "What's the matter? Did the plan change?"

"No," Aden said. "I mean, not as far as I know. I left without telling them, because I overheard them talking. They're worried about how close you seem to Cinderella. I was afraid that if I waited, they would tell me not to bring you the slippers."

A surge of rage went through me—they were *my* slippers, *mine*—followed by a confusing wave of guilt. My sisters weren't entirely wrong, after all.

"Well," I said, "now that you did bring the slippers, I can prove they have nothing to worry about."

I turned back toward the chest. Aden made an odd sound, half throat clearing and half stutter, and I sighed. *"What?"*

He bit the side of his lip, which was red and raw from being chewed on. "I've been thinking a lot about what you said when we left the dungeon. Maybe you were right."

I tried to look smug, and not like I didn't actually remember what I had said in the dungeon.

Aden scuffed his shoe against the floor. "I *did* work hard to convince myself that Dame Yaffa and your sisters were looking out for you. As long as I thought that, I could be your friend and make extra money for my mother and not have to feel guilty about any of it. I needed to believe they were on your side, so I did."

I had to consciously gather enough breath to speak. "And now you think they're not?"

"I don't know. Just because I wanted it to be true, that doesn't make it *not* true." He ran a hand through his hair, leaving it sticking up in short tufts. "But doesn't it seem odd that Dame Yaffa is so willing to give the slippers to someone from your family? She's got to be fae enough to wear them herself. Why doesn't she?"

I tried to remember how small Dame Yaffa's feet were, but I'd never caught a glimpse of them. "She's our godmother. She loved my mother, and now she's trying to take care of us for her sake."

"Maybe you're right," Aden conceded. "Ma says that Dame Yaffa and your mother were best friends."

Somehow, it had never occurred to me until this moment that the adults in the village must have known my mother. My throat was suddenly, ridiculously dry. I remembered a soft hand on my hair, a rumbling laugh against my chest, and the cackling statue on the parade float.

"What else," I said, "did she say about my mother?"

Aden coughed. "Not much. I don't think your mother got along with . . . well, with most people. Ma said she would do anything for her family and for those she loved, but anyone outside that circle meant nothing to her."

He said it like it was a dreadful admission. But wasn't that how everyone was, really? The only difference was that most people weren't forced to pretend that someone they didn't care about was part of their family.

The important thing was that my memories were true. My mother had loved *me*. And this was exactly what she would want: me and my sisters, together, taking back what should always have been ours.

I turned my back on Aden and walked over to the clothes chest. During our conversation, the pull of the slippers had faded even more, but I could still faintly sense the power emanating from the chest.

Which was full of clothes, stacked and neatly folded. That was odd. Did Baro even know how to fold clothes?

A prickly itch crept up the back of my neck—not the pull of the slippers this time, but the sense that something was wrong. I reached into the clothes chest, scooped up as many clothes as I could, and tossed them onto the floor.

"Uh—Tirza?" Aden said. "Gilma is not going to be happy about this."

I flung another armful of clothes behind me.

It wasn't until the chest was empty, its wooden inside

starkly bare, that I admitted to myself what I had known as soon I saw the neatly folded clothes. What I should have known when I noticed the open window.

The slippers were gone.

I could still sense the magic, but it was fainter now. The slippers *had* been here, probably resting right on top of those clothes. I had been feeling the residue of their power.

But someone else had gotten here before me. While I was standing outside the door—or maybe before that, when I was distracted by Baro—someone had taken the slippers, opened that window, and climbed out. Or *flown* out.

I stepped back from the clothes chest. My foot came down on a crumpled silk shirt, which slipped out from under me. I lost my balance and sat down hard on a mass of colorful fabrics.

"Tirza?" Aden said.

I tried to kick the clothes away, but a pair of gloves had gotten wrapped around my ankle.

"What's wrong?" Aden demanded. "Did Baro not hide the slippers here?"

"He did." My voice sounded like it was coming from very far away. "But someone else found them before I got here."

"What do you mean?"

"The slippers were in this chest." I peeled the gloves off my leg. "And now they're gone. Someone took them."

"That's impossible! Who could do that?"

"My guess," I said, "is that it's whoever stole them from the queen's room in the first place." Aden opened his mouth, and I added firmly, "Since that person *wasn't* me."

I couldn't tell what Aden was thinking. Finally, he said, "Right. Then who was it?"

I knew the answer to that question. A part of me had known it since the queen said, *I know how they call to you. They call to me the same way.*

And I should have realized it long before that. Back when the slippers had first disappeared, right after I placed them neatly on the queen's bed.

Because there was, in fact, only one person who could have taken the slippers in those two minutes in that empty room. Everything that everyone had said about the theft was true. It *was* unlikely that someone had dashed in right behind me, stolen the slippers, and gotten away before Queen Ella walked in. Especially since no one had seen that person.

Because that person didn't exist.

Only two people had walked into Queen Ella's room. One of those people had stolen the slippers.

It hadn't been me.

It had been the queen.

26

"I don't understand," Aden said when I was done explaining. "Why would the queen steal her own slippers?"

"Because they're not hers," I said. "They were meant to be mine. When she saw me put them on, she realized it wouldn't be long before I would be able to use them better than she ever could."

And she had been afraid. That was what I had seen in the garden—the tightness in her eyes, the desperation in her voice. *They're dangerous*, she had said.

But it wasn't the slippers that were dangerous. It was me.

I walked to the open window. The metallic scent was stronger here, and I recognized it, even before I saw the patch of dark liquid on the rug. There wasn't that much blood; the slippers would have soaked most of it up before Cinderella put them on her feet and flew out of the room.

She must have been in this room, taking them, while I was standing outside wrestling with my conscience. What an idiot I was.

"She stole them," I said, "to keep me from figuring out how to use them."

"And then she put them in the boat?" Aden asked. "Why?"

"Because it was the last place I would ever look for them."

"Was it, really?" Aden said. "I mean, you wouldn't have looked for them in the horse trough. Or buried in the garden. Or in the queen's underwear drawer. Or—"

"Okay, fine," I said. "I don't know why she put them in the boat. But I know she's the one who took them. She's the *only* one who could have taken them." I looked at the empty clothes chest. "And she just took them again."

She must have sensed their power as soon as they were in the castle. Why hadn't we thought of that before we brought them within her reach?

Esme and Danica had made the same mistake they'd made six years ago. They had underestimated their step-sister. And so had I.

Aden followed my gaze. "So the queen has the slippers now? She's wearing them to the ball? But that means—"

"It means my sisters are walking straight into a trap."

I scrambled to my feet. "I have to get to the ball before they do."

"It's too late, Tirza." Aden stepped jerkily toward the door. "There's nothing you can do to help them, not without the slippers. You need to get out of here."

I knew he was right. But I thought of my sisters walking into that ballroom, expecting me to join them. I imagined their faces when they saw the slippers on Cinderella's feet and realized I was nowhere in sight.

"I have to go to them," I said. "I'm not going to leave them to face her alone."

"That's ... What's the polite word?" Aden considered. "I don't think there is a polite word."

"The word is *loyalty*," I snapped. "You would have no way of knowing this, but there are many people who feel it. Sometimes several times a day."

"Enough." Aden crossed his arms over his chest. "This isn't about what *I* did. I know I was wrong."

"I'm so proud of you. Do you think as long as you admit it, that makes it right?"

"At least I'm honest!"

"Why do you think most people *aren't* honest? It's because if they admit what they're doing is wrong, they'll have to *stop* doing it." I turned my back on him. "Congratulations on finding an easier way around that."

I started toward the door, tripped on some clothes, and managed, after much flailing, to stay upright. As I opened the door, Aden said, "What are you doing?"

"I'm going to the ball. You don't have to come with me."

He was silent for a long, heavy moment before he said, "Good. Because I wasn't planning on it."

Disappointment hit me low in the stomach.

Not that I should have expected any better. After all, every other time I'd told him to save himself—and I was starting to make a habit of it—he had done exactly that.

But I had believed Aden was my friend for almost four years. My gut still expected him to act like my friend, even though my brain knew better.

Well, there went my last illusion. As well as my last chance to give a noble speech.

I walked out of the room and closed the door firmly behind me.

———————◆———————

I made no attempt to hide as I walked through the halls toward the ballroom. I didn't have time to sneak around—and besides, I didn't want to hide.

Or at least, I didn't *want* to want to hide. Which was almost the same thing.

I encountered only a few people: a nobleman with a rip

in his cape and a distraught expression, a maid carrying a pile of fancy gloves, a kitchen girl with a tray of pumpkin tarts. They were all clearly in a rush, but each one of them took the time to stop and stare at me, as if a giant cockroach was marching through the castle.

The ballroom was full of colors and lights, nobles in fancy clothing stepping together on the dance floor and stuffing their faces with food. Three musicians played a popular tune, but they were almost drowned out by the talk and laughter. The tablecloths and napkins were orange, and the air smelled strongly of nutmeg and cinnamon—the ball was always pumpkin-themed, because in one of the minstrel's most popular songs, she claimed Cinderella had traveled to the ball in a coach shaped like a pumpkin.

Queen Ella had told me once that it wasn't true. "I walked all the way. But"—she had lowered her voice— "I *love* everything pumpkin-flavored. Even the royal baker can't mess up a pumpkin pie. So let's not tell anyone, okay?"

I had eaten enough ball leftovers to know that she was dead wrong about that. The royal baker was capable of messing up *anything*. Most of the pumpkin tarts and muffins were untouched. Though the pitchers of pumpkin wine were half empty.

The king and queen sat on the dais, watching the dancers. Queen Ella was wearing her formal crown, the one that gave her a headache—solid gold and made up of long, pointy spikes. She was also wearing a blue gown the exact same shade as mine, and her hem was lifted just high enough to reveal the tip of a glass slipper peeking out from under it.

I thought about turning around and running back to my room. Instead, I took a deep breath and stepped into the ballroom, braced for what would happen.

Nothing happened. No one even looked at me. The dance tune turned lively, and the nobles began twirling in the center of the dance floor. Servants scurried around the room, removing plates and bringing out trays and mopping up spills. One bumped into me, made an annoyed sound, and went on without glancing at me.

It was a bit of a letdown.

But as I crossed the room, a sound started to follow me—soft at first, but growing louder: a shocked, vicious murmur. I did my best to ignore it.

The queen still hadn't glanced in my direction. Nor had the king. They were busy talking to the ambassador from Linderwall. That was good; the Linderwallians were obsessed with dragon-preservation treaties, and it would be a while before they managed to get rid of the ambassador. During that time I could . . .

I came up with nothing. As Aden had pointed out, there wasn't anything I could do. But the good news was I hadn't spotted my sisters. Which meant Cinderella hadn't seen them yet either. If I could get to them before she did, I could at least warn them.

"Tirza!" the minstrel cried. "Why didn't you tell me you were coming? I would have had the musicians play your new song!"

The minstrel had a well-trained voice. It *carried.* All over the ballroom, people turned, including the king and queen. Cinderella put a hand up to indicate to the ambassador that he should stop talking.

"What are you doing here?" a familiar voice demanded, and I whirled to face Gilma. She was standing far too close to me, holding a half-full wineglass in one hand. "Sneaking in to steal something again?"

"What is she stealing?" a voice asked from behind me.

"Is she after the slippers?"

"Who let her escape?"

" '*She walked in all defiant and brave,*' " the minstrel mused, " '*though she had no dignity left to save …*' " She pulled a notepad and pencil out from one of her skirt pockets and began scribbling.

Gilma narrowed her eyes. She was wearing elbow-length white gloves, with a tiny dark spot at the edge of one pinkie. Apparently, she had decided not to change it, which was how she had gotten to the ball before me.

"How dare you show your face here after everything you've done?"

I took a moment of satisfaction in the memory of Gilma's clothes strewn all over her floor.

"You shouldn't be here," she said, and grabbed my wrist with one gloved hand.

"The queen shouldn't have to see her face," a nearby maid agreed. "Not tonight."

"Just because she puts up with her at other times—"

The minstrel was writing frantically. "What did you say?" she asked the nobleman behind her. "Was it *vermin* or *squirming*? I didn't quite catch—"

"What he *said*," Gilma declared, "was that Tirza should have known better than to come to this ball, now that even the queen knows she's a traitor and a thief."

I took a step back, and she smirked at me. Behind her, the nobles nodded. It was like they were about to hold me down and pour dye into my hair.

And just like back then, nothing I said would stop her. Because this wasn't about me—not really. Gilma didn't hate me because of anything I'd done, or because of my family, or even because the queen liked me more than she liked her.

She hated me because she had wronged me, and she knew it. Hating me was easier than feeling guilty about it.

Which meant whatever I did next would make no difference anyhow. So ...

I snatched her wineglass out of her hand and dashed its contents into her face.

I had been aiming for her hair—I *still* remembered what it felt like to have mine turn green—but I wasn't tall enough. The effect was still satisfying. Gilma screamed, putting both hands up to her face. Liquid dripped down her cheeks and off her chin, and when she lowered her hands, the fingers of her gloves were stained deep purple.

"Are you crazy?" she demanded.

"No," I said. "Just wicked."

"Enough!" Queen Ella shouted, standing.

Everyone went silent, except the ambassador. "And the extremely delicate matter of damages for dragon fire ...," he went on, before noticing that everyone could hear him and gulping into silence.

"Tirza," the queen said. She held out a hand. "Come."

I smirked at Gilma, who was using her sodden gloves to try to wipe her face clean. Then I walked through the crowd of disdainful faces.

"I was enjoying the dancing," the queen added forcefully, and the musicians started up again. The dancers went reluctantly back to stepping and twirling, though most of them were staring at me too hard to pay attention. There was a lot of tripping and people bumping into one another.

I paused at the foot of the dais. I couldn't feel the slippers at all, not even the faintest tingle under my skin.

Because Cinderella was soaking up their power. Using it to control the court.

King Ciaran scowled at me. Dozens of equally unfriendly eyes burned into my back. I stepped onto the dais and sank into a reluctant curtsy.

Before I could rise from it fully, Cinderella leaned forward and drew me into a hug.

I went stiff, and she let go. A wrinkle creased her brow. The king looked from her face to mine, and his expression got even darker.

I was glad my sisters hadn't seen that hug.

"I'm sorry," Cinderella said. "I wish we had walked in together the way I planned. But when I went to your room, you were already gone."

"I'm sorry," I said. "I—" I could not think of a single reasonable excuse. "I got nervous."

"You don't have to be nervous. We're going to start over, Tirza. Forget everything that happened at the harbor, forget the slippers—"

"That's not up to you," the king snarled. Not at me, but at the queen. "Do you really believe she *lost* the slippers?"

My eyes widened. I had never before heard the king say a single harsh word to the queen.

"Yes. I do believe her." I had also never seen the queen aim that fierce, haughty expression of hers at her husband. "She is my sister, Ciaran."

"Do you honestly think that matters? She—" The king got control of himself with obvious difficulty. He glared at the ambassador. "Excuse us, please."

"Yes, of course." The ambassador bobbed his head. "But, er, about my request for requiring blunted swords—"

"It's granted," the king cut him off. "As soon as our lawyers approve of it."

The ambassador gave a crestfallen sigh. "Thank you, Your Majesty," he said sadly. He went to the buffet table and poured himself a large drink.

The king turned back to the queen. He lowered his voice. "How can you believe anything she says?"

Were they actually *fighting*? Why wasn't Cinderella using the slippers' power to charm him? What was she using them *for*?

"I won't have her here," the king said through gritted teeth. "I won't let her hurt you again. Call the guard—"

The doors to the ballroom slammed shut.

King Ciaran stopped in midsentence. The dancers went still in a cacophony of rustles that seemed louder than their movements had been. The musicians stopped playing too, a bit more slowly, one flute trailing off alone and then coming to an embarrassed, stuttering stop.

I paid no attention to any of them. I kept my gaze on Cinderella's face, on the way her head jerked sideways toward the sound, on the way the color drained from her face.

So I knew what I would see before I turned around.

"Hello," Danica said. "Sorry to barge in like this, but I believe you forgot my invitation."

27

Danica stood in front of the ballroom doors, dressed in a green gown with long, tight sleeves and a gauzy train. Her hair was coiled in braids that looped and curved around her head, looking distinctly similar to a crown.

Esme and Dame Yaffa stood slightly behind her. Esme was dressed in an equally elaborate gown of midnight blue, but her braids had already escaped into frizzy tangles. Dame Yaffa wore a simple gray dress without a speck of color on it.

Danica advanced into the room, and the nobles drew away to give her a clear path. She walked oddly, in mincing half steps that didn't match her bold stare.

Now I *could* feel the slippers. Energy tingled through my body, as if some of the power was leaking from the queen and brushing against my skin. I tried to think of a way to warn Danica.

"*Cinderella,*" Danica said. "How lovely to see you again. I must say, you've done a fairly good job of washing the ashes out of your hair."

Cinderella sat motionless. The power from the slippers grew stronger, making the air around me shimmer.

I tried to catch Danica's eye and to gesture subtly at Cinderella's feet. But Danica stopped in front of the dais without glancing at me.

"It seems you weren't expecting us," she said. "It must be quite a shock, after all this time when you were getting away with your deception." She drew herself tall. "Will you tell your people the truth, or shall I?"

Cinderella shook her head helplessly, as if in denial. But there was no hope in the motion.

Why? She had the slippers; why didn't she *use* them?

She's too afraid to use the slippers, Danica had said. But my sister was wrong, and I had known it even then. Danica was remembering the timid, frightened girl she had once tormented. But that girl had risen up and seized power, and *I* knew the queen she had become. If Cinderella was wearing the slippers, if she had access to their power, there was no way she would be sitting there looking so pale and helpless.

Which meant . . .

I realized the truth a moment before Danica stepped onto the dais. She lifted her skirt as she did, high enough for us all to see the glass slippers on her feet. The sense of power filled me, making my skin almost dance on my bones.

The slippers weren't clear. They were red as rubies, glistening and shiny, and I smelled the sharp, metallic scent of blood.

Cinderella flinched.

I stared at the queen's stricken face and then down at her feet. The glass that covered them was delicate and clear, and I still felt not a speck of power from them.

Because they had no power to begin with.

Because they were fakes.

Danica turned to the king. "I suppose I'll tell the truth, then," she said. "*Cinderella* lied to you. She's not the one who can draw on the slippers' full power, who can bring magic back to the realm and keep us safe."

She stepped closer to the throne. She was still walking oddly, putting all her weight on her toes. The motion made her heel slip out of the glass shoe, and I gasped. Danica's heel was a mass of red, as if she had taken a slice right off it. Her blood flowed, steadily and continuously, into the glass slippers.

My gasp caught her attention. She turned and held her hand out to me.

"Sister," she said.

Cinderella's indrawn breath was sharp as a blade. Danica whirled back to face her.

"You have no right to sit on that throne," Danica said to Cinderella. "Kneel, so my sisters and I can take our proper place."

She didn't particularly stress *sisters*, but it rang through the room like a bell. My heart twisted, and I waited helplessly for Cinderella to turn to me with betrayal on her face.

Before that could happen, King Ciaran stood. Danica tilted her head toward him, her lips curving into a smile.

"My queen will not kneel to *you*," he said. "Not ever again." He raised his voice. "Guards!"

Danica's smile vanished. Power lashed from the slippers, and King Ciaran flew sideways off the dais. He crashed into a buffet table, knocking it over with a deafening clash. Plates and food went flying, and the room filled with screams. The king landed on the floor and lay still.

"Ciaran!" Cinderella cried, half rising. Danica whirled and struck her on the side of her face. The blow sent Cinderella sprawling. She landed on the marble floor with a thud.

Esme let out a shrill, high-pitched sound, somewhere between a scream and a laugh.

Cinderella dragged herself to a sitting position and lifted her chin, her cheek bright red. I started toward her, then stopped and turned to my sisters. "Danica, stop! You don't need to hurt her."

"Tirza," Esme said. "Don't—"

Danica held up a hand, and Esme gulped into silence.

"Stay out of this," Danica said to me. "You obviously can't handle what has to be done. That's why I'm taking care of it myself."

"You told me you couldn't wear the slippers!" I said.

"I didn't know I could." Danica smiled at me almost kindly. "It didn't work last time. But Dame Yaffa showed me how I could make them fit. It took some courage, that's all."

She must have sliced half the flesh off her heel. I stared at her in horror and then whirled to Dame Yaffa. "You said *I* was the one who would wear the slippers."

Behind her, two noblemen rushed to the king. Everyone else in the ballroom seemed frozen.

"I lied." Dame Yaffa's smile was less kind than my sister's. "Or rather, I *hoped* it would be you. You're the one the slippers fit, without the need for any messy alterations. But once I met you, I started doubting whether I could count on you. And after your weakness in the woods . . . I knew I had to explore other options." She tilted her head sideways. "Your sisters did try to argue with me, if that makes you feel better. But once I snuck them into the castle and they saw you parading through the halls in Cinderella's dress, they knew I was right." She folded her arms over her chest. "I took them straight to where the slippers were, and we flew away with them when we heard you outside the door. *Danica* wasn't afraid to give them her blood."

"We don't blame you, Tirza," Esme put in. "You've been trapped by Cinderella too long to see her clearly. You still think there's goodness in her." She lifted her hand, as if to reach for me, but then dropped it to her side. "It's not your fault. You can't help believing something you've been told over and over since you were five years old."

The two noblemen were kneeling beside the king. Cinderella got to her feet and said, "Ciaran?"

"He's all right," one of the noblemen said. "He's breathing."

"Good," Danica said, turning. "We're going to need him eventually." She lifted one hand, palm out, and the doors flew open. "Everyone else. *Get out.*"

I found myself taking two steps back, off the dais and away from my sisters. I fought against the compulsion, made myself stop, then felt my foot slide backward despite my best efforts.

"Not you," Danica said to me, and I stopped moving.

"I need my sisters with me." She turned to Dame Yaffa. "And my godmother, of course." Her eyes moved on to Cinderella. "And *you*."

The king remained motionless on the ground, but everyone else streamed toward the doors. Some, like the minstrel, were practically running, but many tried to fight. A few of the guards actually grabbed the door-posts in order to hold themselves back. Gilma was one of the last to leave, her feet sliding slowly across the floor, her gloved fists clenched with the effort.

But none of them could stand against the slippers' power. As soon as the last guard was forced through the doorway, Danica waved her hand at the doors, and they slammed shut. The crossbar dropped into place with a resounding thud.

"Well," Danica said into the sudden silence. "Now it's just family. Four sisters and our godmother. Isn't that nice? If only our mother could be here too." She lifted her skirt and descended the dais steps, stalking toward Cinderella.

The slippers on her feet weren't red anymore; they were crystal clear, glittering in the lights from the ballroom's chandeliers. They had soaked up all that blood and turned it into power.

"Danica," I said. "Don't hurt her."

Esme grabbed my hand and squeezed.

"Calm down, little sister," Danica said. "I'm not going to kill her, since it would bother you so much. I'll just exile her the same way she did us." She flicked a finger at her stepsister.

Cinderella's elegant gown vanished, leaving her wearing only a shift. Danica snapped her fingers, and a dark cloud appeared in the air above Cinderella's head, raining a gray mist onto her hair. It smelled faintly burnt—

Ashes, I realized as the cloud vanished. They clung to Cinderella's shift, covered her hair, and smudged her face. She knelt in a pile of them, yet somehow managed to look at Danica with that haughty, superior expression I hated.

Recognition flashed through me. I had seen that look so many times on the queen—but before that, a long time ago, I had seen it on that wan, dirty face. When Cinderella should have been defeated, should have been cowed, she had always managed to look up with that fierce, defiant pride.

It had always enraged Danica, and clearly, that had not changed. Danica actually gnashed her teeth as she thrust her hand outward.

Cinderella flew backward across the room and thudded to a stop in the corner.

"Danica," I tried again. "Please—"

"Be *quiet*!" Esme said. "Whose side are you on?"

Cinderella struggled to her knees, lifted her head, and glared haughtily across the room.

Translucent blue fire writhed between Danica's fingers. She thrust her hand at Cinderella, and the surge of power from the slippers was so strong I felt it through my bones.

I lunged across the space between us, jerking free of Esme and slamming into Danica. We tumbled to the floor together, and the blast of power Danica had been aiming at Cinderella hit one of the chandeliers instead. It shattered, raining glass on us. Sharp prickles of pain erupted all over my skin.

Danica snarled in fury, and the pressure in the air turned into a vast wind. It lifted me and threw me backward, into the corner where Cinderella crouched. I slammed into her as I landed, and a sprinkle of ashes fell over my hair and face.

Danica swept her arm in a half circle. A line of fire shot up in front of me, forming a bright, hot barrier that trapped me and Cinderella in the corner.

Danica got to her feet. The glass had nicked her too; a thin line of blood snaked down her right leg and vanished into the eager glass slipper.

"See?" she said to Esme. "I told you not to trust her." She turned to face me, lifting both hands. The now-hot wind flung me back against the wall, lashing my hair into my face like a thousand tiny whips.

Danica's lips were drawn back, her eyes blazing, and she looked at me exactly the same way she had looked at Cinderella.

"I suppose I should thank you, Tirza," she said, "for making it clear where you stand. Now that we don't have to worry about your delicate feelings, I can finish this."

28

Wind whirled through the air. The broken chandeliers swayed and shuddered, and shards of glass rained over the room, landing in the abandoned plates and on the empty dance floor. Some of them fell on Danica's hair, but she didn't seem to notice. She threw her head back, her hair glittering, a nimbus of blue fire glowing all around her.

Esme stared at me, stricken. I turned my head away. But then I found myself looking at Cinderella, which was even worse.

"Cin— *Ella.*" That was what I had called her, once upon a time, though only when my sisters couldn't hear. When they were around, I had called her Cinderella like they had. Had teased and taunted her like they had. Had been taught wickedness and cruelty, and never admitted to myself that I had learned it. Instead, I had seen it in the person I had tormented. It had been easier than feeling guilt. "I'm *sorry*."

Cinderella shook her head. "It's my fault. If I had told you the truth, if I had trusted you to understand, then none of this would have happened. You would never have stolen the slippers to begin with."

I blinked at her.

"I didn't do it," I said.

It had been a while since I said it, but the words still felt futile, worn smooth by repetition.

"Tirza." Her expression was haughty despite the dirt staining it. She was still holding on to her pride—which she must have struggled so desperately to keep, during those years when she was mocked and tormented, when everyone thought she was nothing. "I told you I forgive you. I should have—"

"Are you saying," I interrupted her, "that *you* didn't steal the slippers?"

"Of course I didn't steal them!"

"Neither did I." I forced myself to my feet. "So *who did*?"

On the other side of the flames, Danica rose into the air. Her hair billowed around her, and her entire body was . . . Was it *glowing*?

I couldn't tell. But there was *something* unnatural

about her as she stretched her arms to the side, blue flames still dancing around them.

Okay, there were a couple of unnatural things about her.

"Say goodbye!" she said, and laughed.

I definitely wasn't imagining it. Her laugh wasn't quite human. It was like the slippers' magnetic pull had been translated into sound.

A wind roared through the room, hitting me full in the face and pushing me back into the wall. It was so strong and hot I gasped for breath. Across the room, a buffet table blew over, silverware and plates clattering across the floor.

"Danica!" Dame Yaffa said. "Keep it under control!"

"I *am*!" The glass in the windows shattered, one by one, and the cool night air whipped into the room. "I can do *anything*!"

Her skirt wrapped around her legs, revealing the slippers. They were blindingly bright, pulsing with power. *That* was the source of the glow spreading under Danica's skin.

"Stop!" I screamed, but the wind snatched the words from my mouth. "Danica, you need to stop! The slippers are draining you—"

Danica's laughter pealed around the room, and her skin shimmered, as if little motes of glass were lodged under it and reflecting the lights of the shattered chandeliers.

"You can't reach her." The queen was right next to me, but her voice was almost drowned out by the wind. "The slippers have her. I've seen it before. Nothing could induce her to take them off."

"But she'll—" I broke off.

"She'll die," Cinderella finished for me. Her voice was low and grim. "Like your mother died when she tried to draw on the slippers' power. This is what I've been trying to prevent all this time. I was afraid—" Her voice broke. "I was afraid it would be you."

So she had kept me away from the slippers, and done everything she could to get them away from me once I had them.

"Dame Yaffa!" I shouted.

Dame Yaffa turned to face me, and my plea died in my throat. She didn't seem to mind the wind slashing at her dress and ripping her hair from its bun. Her eyes gleamed exultantly.

Why doesn't she wear them herself? Aden had asked, and the answer was now obvious. The slippers were dangerous. They had killed my mother, and they were killing my sister. Of course Dame Yaffa preferred to let others take that risk. She didn't have to try to control the slippers if she could control the people wearing them.

 235

"Da—" My voice was pushed back into my throat by the wind. I couldn't draw in breath, and panic spiraled through the tightness in my chest. Danica pointed in my direction, and the blue fire surrounding her flared so bright I couldn't see her face.

But I heard her scream, just as the wind died all at once.

I jerked my head up and met Danica's wide, startled eyes in the second between her scream and her fall. In the sudden stillness, she made a loud, awful *thump* as she hit the floor.

Esme scrabbled backward, gripping the slippers with both hands.

"You idiot!" Dame Yaffa shrieked, and in the few seconds it took me to catch up with what had happened—to realize that Esme had reached up and pulled the slippers right off Danica's feet—Dame Yaffa swooped forward, backhanded Esme with such force that she fell over, and snatched the slippers from her hands. "That fall might have killed your sister!"

Esme stared up at Dame Yaffa, and then she began to sob.

Dame Yaffa strode over to one of the remaining upright tables, the slippers dangling from her hand. She picked up a knife.

Cinderella scrambled to her feet and stepped toward

her. But the fire in front of us flared up, the heat unbearable, and she stopped.

Dame Yaffa tested the edge of the knife with her finger. She put it down and stalked down the table, looking for a sharper one.

"Give me your crown!" I said to Cinderella. "Quick!"

Cinderella whipped her head around. After only a second of hesitation, she yanked the crown from her head and handed it to me.

I didn't allow myself to hesitate for even a second. I turned the crown upside down and scraped one of its sharp points hard across my calf.

The wound where I had been bitten had barely started healing. It opened at once, blood gushing out.

Just like my blood had spurted from the cut made by the tarp, right before the slippers appeared in the boat.

No one had hidden them in the boat. Just like no one had taken them from the queen's bed, back when all this had started.

I finally understood who had stolen the slippers. It hadn't been the queen. It hadn't been my sisters.

It had, in the end, been me.

All I had done was dance in them for a few minutes. But the slippers had been desperate. That had given them enough power to remove *themselves* from the cage Cinderella had put them in.

I hadn't needed them then, so they had vanished—away from Cinderella and this castle, where they had been contained for so long. But they had become connected to me, so when I needed them—when I was terrified and needed to draw on their power—they had come to *me*, drawn by my fear and my blood.

And they would do it again.

As soon as the blood poured down my leg, I felt the slippers' response; not just in my skin this time, but all through my body, a painful and glorious burst of magic. The feeling was so overwhelming that I couldn't see. I heard Dame Yaffa's shriek of rage as the slippers tore themselves from her grip, and then the smooth glass curves of the slippers were in my hand, and my blood came alive.

"TIRZA!" Esme screamed.

I looked up, seeing the room through a dazzle of crystalline light.

Danica lay on the floor, her skirt hiked up around her knees, revealing her blood-splattered feet. Esme was draped over her, sobbing and screaming—basically a run-through of everyone's names: *Danica! Dame Yaffa! Tirza!*

Dame Yaffa crouched on the floor, her arm extended, her fingers clawed; she had tried and failed to grab the slippers. She stood, snatched a knife from the table, and spun to face me.

"You did this!" Dame Yaffa pointed at Danica's prone body. "You killed your sister!"

Esme let out a long, piercing sob. But Danica stirred and coughed, which kind of ruined the moment.

Relief swept through me. Because even if I had chosen to side against my sisters . . . they were still my sisters.

"She might not be dead yet," Dame Yaffa snapped, as if Danica was showing signs of life just to irritate her. "But she *will* be! What do you think Cinderella will do to her now? Or to *you*?"

"I'm not afraid of the queen," I said. And it was true; I wasn't. I never had been. I had only been able to call the slippers at times when I really thought I was in danger— when the village boys surrounded me, in the dungeon when I had been afraid of Baro's reaction, at the harbor when I had seen the king aim an arrow at me. Never when my opponent was the queen.

Because deep down, I had always known she wouldn't hurt me.

Dame Yaffa started toward me, then whirled and dashed sideways. She grabbed Esme by the hair, pulled her off Danica, and put the knife to her throat.

Esme shrieked, a long despairing wail with no names or words in it at all.

"Quiet," Dame Yaffa growled, and Esme gulped into sudden silence.

"Well, Tirza?" Dame Yaffa said. "How far are you willing to take your betrayal? Will you let another of your sisters die in order to hold on to those slippers?"

Danica groaned and lifted her head. Dame Yaffa shot her another annoyed look.

"Tirza," Esme whispered, her eyes wide with terror. The knife blade was pressed right against her throat. "Please."

"Give me the slippers," Dame Yaffa said. "Now."

"What are you going to do with them?" I demanded. The slippers' deadly, compelling power tingled against my hands. I kicked off my satin shoes. "Slash off half of Esme's heel, like you did to Danica?"

Dame Yaffa's lip curled. "Esme isn't strong enough. And maybe I'm tired of giving that power to other people. You've all been so tiresomely ungrateful and disobedient. I think it's time for that power to be mine."

"You don't dare," I said. "That's why you've always tried to control the people who wear them, because you know you can't control the slippers themselves. They'll take everything you have."

"Maybe so," Dame Yaffa said. "And then you'll be rid of me, won't you? So give them to me."

"Tirza," Esme squeaked.

The slippers thrummed under my fingers. I wanted to put them on more than I had ever wanted anything in my life. What I had sensed the first time I touched them, a shimmer of possibility, was now a brilliant, awe-inspiring blaze.

Once I put them on, Dame Yaffa would be nothing to me. I could save Cinderella *and* Esme *and* Danica—all the family I had left. I could make everything right again.

Something brushed against my arm. Cinderella, grabbing my shoulder.

Cinderella. The one person who had been able to dance in the slippers and hold them at bay; to control her desire for power, even after all the years in that cottage, when she must have wanted power more than anything.

"Don't," Cinderella said. "Don't put them on, Tirza. You'll never be able to take them off."

The wild thrill of magic ran through me. My skin felt too tight.

"The second they touch your foot," Dame Yaffa warned, "your sister dies." But her voice trembled slightly, a hint of fear I had never heard from her before.

She won't really do it, I thought. *She'll say anything to stop me. But in a second, I'll stop her.*

I curled my hand around the heel of the slipper, and then I turned and threw it with all my might.

It hit the wall and broke with a crash that hurt like ice going through me. I screamed, and behind me, I heard

Cinderella doing the same—Cinderella, who had been giving the slippers her life force for years.

Quickly, before the pain could make me too afraid, I flung the other slipper away. My throw was weaker this time—but the slippers were, after all, made of glass. The second one shattered just like the first.

Dame Yaffa shoved Esme away and ran across the room, still holding the knife. She dropped to her knees on top of the glass shards. Blood welled up where the glass cut her, and red drops fell on one of the slippers' pieces, but they slid right off the glass onto the floor.

"You fool," Dame Yaffa snarled. She got to her feet, ignoring the blood running down her legs. "You little *idiot*! Do you know what you've done?"

I was still trembling from the aftereffects of what I had done. I felt like I had broken something inside myself.

The lines of fire shrank and died, robbed of the magic that had been fueling them. Nothing stood between me and Dame Yaffa, who was striding toward us, her face contorted with rage.

Cinderella's strong, slender fingers closed around my hand. The ballroom seemed darker and grayer than it had a moment ago, all the sparkle drained out of it.

The queen and I were trapped in a corner, and only Dame Yaffa had a blade.

I clung to her hand, and she squeezed back, and we waited, helpless, as Dame Yaffa advanced.

The ballroom doors burst open. A battering ram held by a dozen guards crashed through the open doors into the room and slammed into one of the tables. The table splintered into wooden pieces, sending yet more plates and food skidding along the floor.

"Good job!" Aden shouted, dashing past the men into the room. "Save the queen!"

The guards dropped the battering ram—it thudded to the floor so heavily it cracked the marble—and, in identical motions, drew their swords.

Dame Yaffa whirled, still gripping the knife, her gray dress flaring around her.

Gilma burst in through the doors after Aden. Twenty nobles stampeded into the ballroom behind her, holding . . . I blinked. Were those butter knives?

Well, it was the thought that counted.

"Step away from our queen!" Gilma said.

Dame Yaffa focused on Aden. Her eyes narrowed. "Traitor," she spat.

Aden lifted a shoulder. "So what else is new?"

Dame Yaffa lifted the knife, pointed it at the floor, and dropped it. It landed with a clang.

"I am not your enemy," she said. "Open your eyes, people of Tarel. Queen Ella is cruel and vicious. She'll turn on you all if you don't take this chance to finally stop her!"

I opened my mouth, but I had no chance to speak. The laughter that filled the room was too loud.

Beside me, Cinderella drew herself up. With the ashes on her hair and covering her ragged, fire-singed shift, she should have looked like the pathetic servant girl she had once been. Instead, she looked like she had been born to be queen.

Dame Yaffa turned and ran.

She was so fast that no one had a chance to stop her before she reached one of the large windows. She looked back into the room once, her eyes black and cold, then threw herself through the gaping hole in the shattered glass.

"*No!*" Cinderella and Esme cried together.

Cinderella raced to the window, glass crunching beneath her shoes. I followed as fast as I could on bare feet. Together we stared out through the jagged-edged hole in the windowpane.

Below us was an empty rocky cliff, and beyond that, the sea. There was no sign of Dame Yaffa anywhere.

The slippers aren't my only source of magic, she had told us on the beach.

Cinderella put her arm around me. I stiffened, but she didn't pull away; and when she turned, I turned with her.

We stood together facing the chaotic ballroom and the stunned faces of everyone in it.

Danica had dragged herself into a sitting position. She focused on me and Cinderella, and her eyes narrowed. Esme watched us, too, her eyes filled with tears. I forced myself not to avoid their gazes, and also not to slip out from under Cinderella's arm.

"Your Majesty," the captain of the guard said. "What shall we do with them?"

"Execute them, of course," King Ciaran said. The king had also struggled into a sitting position. His eyes were slightly unfocused, but his voice was clear. "We won't make the same mistake as last time."

I looked up at Cinderella, and for the first time, I let the pain inside me spill over my eyes, into tears that she and the whole court could see.

She turned to the king. "They're no danger to us anymore," she said. "And they are still my sisters. Send them back into exile."

"No," the king said. "Not this time, Ella."

Everyone in the room seemed to hold their breaths.

"Tirza saved all our lives," the queen said in a clear, ringing voice. "After we falsely accused her, she risked herself to save us. This is her only request. Are you really going to deny her?"

A murmur of agreement rose from the butter

 245

knife–wielding nobles. Gilma opened her mouth, as if to argue, then looked around, flushed, and pressed her lips together.

The king let out a heavy breath.

"No," he said. "I suppose we cannot."

Danica limped heavily as she was led out of the ballroom, and she refused to look at me. When they reached the door, Esme started to turn in my direction. But Danica grabbed her wrist, and Esme kept looking straight ahead.

I waited until my sisters were gone, and then I turned to my stepsister. Ella smiled down at me, and I saw the warmth and relief in that smile . . . and something more than that, something that made my heart expand and lift. Something that surprised but also thrilled me, that had been there all along but that I had refused to pay attention to.

"You know," I said, "that's not going to be my *only* request."

Ella laughed and reached for my hand. Together, we walked across the ballroom to greet her subjects.

➤ EPILOGUE ◄

"I'm still not sure this is a good idea," Ella said.

I rolled my eyes. Admittedly, I did it while facing forward so my sister couldn't see. Ella can be prickly when people are dismissive of her.

Not that I blame her.

"I am sure," I said. Our boat rose and fell on the white-rimmed waves. Far ahead, the Larosian cliffs carved a stark black outline against the sky. "Even the king thinks we should do this. If me and King Ciaran agree on something, how can it *not* be right?"

Ella laughed. She hooked her finger under a lock of my wind-strewn hair and tucked it behind my ear. "Good point. But don't you have any doubts, Tirza? Once we do this, they'll be gone forever."

I picked up the velvet bag nestled in the bottom of the boat. A tingle started at the edge of my skin, a subtle energy that emanated from the glass pieces in that small black bag.

 247

I ignored the tingle. It shouldn't have been there; I had felt the slippers' power shatter when I broke them that night at the ball, four months ago. And I had felt the emptiness in the glass pieces afterward, when Ella and I gathered them up together.

The two of us had cleaned the ballroom on our own that night; we didn't trust anyone else to do it. We had talked nonstop while we cleaned, and then for the rest of the night. There were so many memories we each had only pieces of, so many misunderstandings and resentments between us. We had barely gotten a start on getting through them, but we had been working on it almost every day since. Ella was busier than ever, but we had breakfast together several times a week and occasional walks in the garden after dinner.

Four months was a long time. Long enough for us to be almost easy together, for me to see where her sore spots were and learn not to rub against them. Long enough for Esme and Danica to be packed off to an even more distant exile. Long enough for me to write them letters, though I hadn't sent them yet. I wouldn't do that without asking Ella, in case she saw dangers that I didn't. Or in case she wanted to add a letter of her own.

And long enough for the slippers to recover from their shattering and start drawing on their power again? Maybe. Which was why we had to do this.

Aden was the only one who disagreed. He was fixated on how much money the kingdom could make by selling fragments of the slippers to tourists and magicians. He had prepared an entire presentation on the issue, which I had convinced Ella to listen to, and which had ended with the ringing line, "Now that we don't have magic, we must focus on staying strong through trade!"

He hadn't convinced Ella to go along with his suggestion. But she *had* removed him from his stable boy duties and put him in the ministry of finance. He was rising rapidly through the ranks there, at least according to him.

Then Gilma pointed out that it didn't really matter if we had the slippers' magic. What mattered was that people *thought* we had it.

Which was why Ella and I had to do this alone.

The only people who knew we were here tonight were Aden, the king, and Gilma, and we trusted all three of them—even if two of the three didn't exactly trust *me*. But the king, I thought, was coming around. He knew how important I was to Ella, and protecting her was the only thing that mattered to him more than the needs of the kingdom.

Gilma, on the other hand, would never like me. The feeling was entirely mutual. But I couldn't doubt her loyalty to the queen, and we had learned to cooperate in the all-important endeavor of avoiding each other as much as possible. It was a lot easier now that the princes had graduated to a governess, and Gilma had been assigned to assist the royal hairdresser.

Besides, Gilma was hardly alone in her feelings. Most people in the castle still believed I stole the slippers. The queen was working on changing their minds. Personally, I didn't think she would succeed until she sent the minstrel away. But I also, these days, found it easier not to care.

The ocean stretched around us, so black it merged seamlessly with the sky and with the far-off cliffs of the peninsula. The moon was a pale smudge covered by shifting clouds. Ella reached for my hand and gripped it, and I squeezed back. The wind whipped our hair back and blew the clouds away from the moon, giving enough light to see the triangular fin that rose out of the water and then disappeared back into it.

"Sharks," I noted, trying to keep my voice calm.

Ella followed my gaze and smiled. She had a ridiculous regard for animals; I had yet to break it to her that, unlike her, I didn't find the mice in my room cute. "Just bluefish. They're nothing to worry about."

"Actually," I muttered, "their teeth are *very* sharp."

Ella let go of my hand and took up the oars. "Ready?"

I leaned over the side of the boat and tilted the bag sideways. The waves surged higher, as if trying to carry the glass shards away. But the fragments dropped into the water, a glittering cascade, and disappeared with tiny plinks into the sea.

Ella was *good* at rowing. Someday, I'd have to ask her how she had picked up that skill. For now, I let the glass shards trickle out as slowly as I could while her oars shot the boat through the swells.

One of the shards slid along my fingers, and this time I *definitely* wasn't imagining it. Magic and possibility shot through me, a stab of longing. Without thinking, I started to pull the bag upright and draw it closed.

But Ella said quietly, "Tirza."

I let my breath out and tilted the bag, and the last shards of the glass slippers slid into the sea. The froth seemed a little sharper, a little brighter, than it had before, and the waves soared the tiniest bit higher before they smashed themselves against the side of our boat.

Though that part, probably, *was* my imagination.

I held the bag out for a second longer, just in case some tiny fragments were left, but mostly because I didn't want the moment to end. Not yet.

Ella's hair brushed my shoulder as she leaned sideways, digging deep with one oar to turn the boat around. The waves swelled around us, and our craft tilted but held steady, skimming through the sparkling dark water and bringing us back home.

Acknowledgments

Thank you to:

My amazing family: my husband, children, parents, in-laws, and siblings. This year strained our bonds in ways we could never have imagined but also proved that we remain connected no matter what.

My writing community, including and especially Diana Peterfreund, Sarah Beth Durst, Andrea Pawley, and Erin Roberts.

The members of OLUF, for being willing to cheerfully answer all my random questions.

As always, I wrote this book with the help of many critique partners and sounding boards. Thank you, Christine Amsden, Kit Aronoff, Chanie Beckman, Devora Gorfajn, Eliezer Gorfajn, Sol Kim Bentley, Rina Peromsik, Tova Suslovich, Bela Unell, Liza Wiemer, and Fran Wilde.

This time around, the most important critiques came from my own children—Shoshana and Hadassah, each of whom listened to me read the whole book from beginning to end. (I forgive you for turning down that third reading.)

Though I haven't seen my cover yet, I can't wait, because I know I'm going to love it! And I know I'll have Carol Ly and Kelsey Eng to thank for that.

Last but not least: my agent, Andrea Somberg (who functions as critique partner, support group, and advocate all at once); my incredible editor, Wendy Loggia; my eagle-eyed copyeditor, Jeannie Ng; and all the wonderful people at Delacorte Press, especially Ali Romig and Lili Feinberg.

Did you know Sleeping Beauty had a little sister?

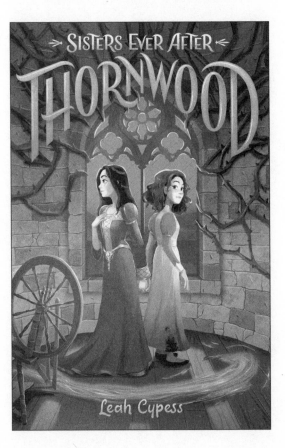

These are the adventures of the siblings who never made it into the storybook.

1

I've always known what would happen to my sister on her sixteenth birthday. Her doom has been hanging over her head since before I was born.

So when I woke that morning, I went straight to her room.

It was before sunrise, so Rosalin was still alone. Soon everyone would descend upon her—her ladies-in-waiting, our parents, the royal wizard. This was the day she would be struck down by her curse—the spell that, even more than her astonishing beauty, made her the center of attention everywhere she went. Today would be like every other day of her life, except a million times more intense.

And nobody but me would know how much she hated it.

From the door, my sister looked like she was still asleep, her head turned to the side and her breathing soft and even. But Rosalin is the one who taught *me* how to fake being asleep. I wasn't fooled.

I padded across the room, past delicate wooden tables piled with birthday gifts, and hopped up onto her bed.

"Hi," I said.

She didn't move. She didn't open her eyes.

"Come on," I said. "*Today*, of all days, you want to pretend to be asleep?"

Rosalin's eyes popped open, then narrowed. "That is an incredibly insensitive thing to say! What is wrong with you?" She pulled herself to a sitting position and snorted. "Aside from your hair, I mean."

I touched my hair instinctively. I hadn't brushed it before I came—not that it would have been less of a frizzy tangle if I had.

"And your face. You have chocolate on your *eyelashes*, Briony. How did you even manage that?"

She knew how I had managed it. We had sat up late last night going through her boxes of birthday chocolates, laughing and stuffing ourselves and arguing over who got the cream-filled ones.

Yet somehow, even though I hadn't left until she was nearly asleep—when I knew my plan to distract her had worked—Rosalin's face this morning was smooth and clear, unmarred by the slightest hint of exhaustion or chocolate.

"It got you up, didn't it?" I said. "We need to talk before everyone else gets here. You're going to make sure you're never alone today, right?"

Rosalin's face went tight. "Yes, Briony. I will have one of my ladies accompany me everywhere. I'm sure that's all it will take to defeat a fairy curse."

I winced. I wasn't used to hearing her refer to the curse out loud—even though everyone in the castle, everyone in the *kingdom*, knew what was supposed to happen to her today.

On the day she turns sixteen, she will prick her finger on a spinning wheel and fall asleep. She will sleep for one hundred years, and the entire castle will sleep with her. The curse will be broken only when a brave and noble prince fights his way through the thorns around the castle and wakes her with a kiss.

And that was better than her original fate. The curse the fairy queen had put on my parents, long ago, had said that their firstborn daughter would be beautiful, but would prick her finger and die on her sixteenth birthday. Rosalin's fairy godmother had managed to change the curse from *die* to *sleep for a hundred years*, which was an improvement, but still not exactly ideal.

No one knew why the fairy queen was so angry at my parents. Supposedly it was because they hadn't invited her to their wedding, but it had been decades since the fairies had attended any royal parties. According to the court minstrel, it was the fairy queen herself who had commanded that all fairies withdraw from the human world and stop meddling in human affairs. My parents had assumed inviting them was just a formality, and they hadn't gotten around to it.

And then the fairy queen had taken offense and cursed their first child.

I wanted to reach for Rosalin's hand, but the way she held herself—like her body was made of porcelain—told me she would slap me away if I tried.

"The guards have been pulling extra patrols for weeks," I said. "There's not a single spinning wheel left in the kingdom." Now I was just parroting what my father said. "You're going to be all right, Rosalin. Really."

She did her best to smile, but she didn't meet my eyes.

In my fantasies, I was always coming up with plans to save her. Ways to lift the curse and change everything. Sometimes I dreamed that I bargained with the fairy queen to place the curse solely on me and spare the rest of the castle. I imagined everyone gathered around my sleeping form, amazed at my sacrifice, while Rosalin thanked me through her tears.

I wasn't sure, deep down, that I was brave enough to sacrifice myself to save my sister. But I liked to think I was.

"Rosalin—" I began.

The door flew open, and half a dozen ladies-in-waiting poured into the room, arms full of ribbons and cloth. They fluttered around the bed, and Rosalin pasted a far more convincing smile on her face for their benefit.

Their gazes slid right past me. I pushed myself off the bed, and one of the ladies stepped on my foot.

"Ouch!" I said. She sighed heavily, annoyed that my foot had been in her way.

They gathered my sister up and swept her in the direction of the bath. I stood staring after them until she was out of sight, but Rosalin didn't look back at me even once.

I trudged back toward my room, to rouse my own ladies and convince them that I had to get ready for the party, too.

As far as I could recall, that was the last thing I did that day. That year. That century.

About the Author

Leah Cypess is the author of *Thornwood*, the first book in the Sisters Ever After series, which *Kirkus Reviews* calls "effervescent, thrilling, and practically perfect in every way." She lives in the kingdom of Silver Spring, Maryland, with her family, and never borrows shoes without asking permission first.

leahcypess.com